"Catie," He Groaned, Then Covered Her Mouth With His.

His tongue seared hers and she moaned low in her throat. It was all the encouragement he needed to drag her body against his and close his arms around her.

He remembered the first time he'd made love to her. She'd been a virgin and unsure of what to expect. But she'd also been eager to learn and just as eager to please him.

And one of the times they'd made love, she'd conceived his son.

The thought flitted through Jake's mind, clearing the way for rational thinking. He lifted his head and stared at Catherine's face. She licked at her lips, and the action made his knees want to buckle.

"This doesn't change anything," he growled, angry at himself for touching her. Angry, also, because he wanted to kiss her again.

Dear Reader,

Happy New Year from Silhouette Desire, where we offer you six passionate, powerful and provocative romances every month of the year! Here's what you can indulge yourself with this January....

Begin the new year with a seductive MAN OF THE MONTH, *Tall, Dark & Western* by Anne Marie Winston. A rancher seeking a marriage of convenience places a personals ad for a wife, only to fall—hard—for the single mom who responds!

Silhouette Desire proudly presents a sequel to the wildly successful in-line continuity series THE TEXAS CATTLEMAN'S CLUB. This exciting *new* series about alpha men on a mission is called TEXAS CATTLEMAN'S CLUB: LONE STAR JEWELS. Jennifer Greene's launch book, *Millionaire M.D.*, features a wealthy surgeon who helps out his childhood crush when she finds a baby on her doorstep—by marrying her!

Alexandra Sellers continues her exotic miniseries SONS OF THE DESERT with one more irresistible sheikh in *Sheikh's Woman*. THE BARONS OF TEXAS miniseries by Fayrene Preston returns with another feisty Baron heroine in *The Barons of Texas: Kit*. In Kathryn Jensen's *The Earl's Secret,* a British aristocrat romances a U.S. commoner while wrestling with a secret. And Shirley Rogers offers *A Cowboy, a Bride & a Wedding Vow,* in which a cowboy discovers his secret child.

So ring in the new year with lots of cheer and plenty of red-hot romance, by reading all six of these enticing love stories.

Enjoy!

Joan Marlow Golan

Joan Marlow Golan
Senior Editor, Silhouette Desire

Please address questions and book requests to:
Silhouette Reader Service
U.S.: 3010 Walden Ave., P.O. Box 1325, Buffalo, NY 14269
Canadian: P.O. Box 609, Fort Erie, Ont. L2A 5X3

A Cowboy, a Bride
& a Wedding Vow
SHIRLEY ROGERS

Published by Silhouette Books

America's Publisher of Contemporary Romance

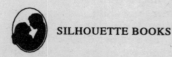

SILHOUETTE BOOKS

ISBN 0-373-76344-1

A COWBOY, A BRIDE & A WEDDING VOW

Copyright © 2001 by Shirley Rogerson

This edition published by arrangement with Harlequin Books S.A.

® and TM are trademarks of Harlequin Books S.A., used under license.
Trademarks indicated with ® are registered in the United States Patent
and Trademark Office, the Canadian Trade Marks Office and in other
countries.

Visit Silhouette at www.eHarlequin.com

Printed in U.S.A.

Books by Shirley Rogers

Silhouette Desire

Cowboys, Babies and Shotgun Vows #1176
Conveniently His #1266
A Cowboy, a Bride & a Wedding Vow #1344

SHIRLEY ROGERS

lives in Virginia with her husband, two cats and an adorable Maltese named Blanca. She has two grown children, a son and a daughter. As a child, she was known for having a vivid imagination. It wasn't until she started reading romances that she realized her true destiny was writing them! Besides reading, she enjoys traveling and going to the movies.

Shirley loves to hear from readers. Please enclose a self-addressed, stamped envelope and write to: PMB#189, 1920-125 Centerville Tpke., Virginia Beach, VA 23464.

To my father,
Frank Steadman, Jr.
1921-2000
I miss you.

One

"**I** think you're my father."

Jake McCall stood stock-still and sucked in a hard breath. His heart began to pound, causing a roaring in his ears that resembled the rumbling sound of cattle being herded on his family's remote Texas ranch. As he stared back at the tall, lanky youth on his porch, Jake's face was blank. He couldn't possibly have heard right.

No way.

I think you're my father.

The words reverberated through Jake's mind, robbing him of an immediate coherent response. He fought for lucidity as he tried to make sense of what he'd just heard. His eyebrows drawn together, Jake shook his head, searched for his voice and stated quite emphatically, "I believe you're mistaken, son."

His tone was deep and firm, his eyes steady as his

gaze studied the disheveled kid. He was dressed in faded jeans that rode low on his hips and looked at least two sizes too big, as did his white T-shirt, spattered with what Jake thought must be the name of some rock group. The thick layer of road dust on the boy's Nike sneakers nearly hid their black color. His brown hair was well below his collar.

Jake met the kid's guarded expression as he shifted his backpack from his shoulder. He caught it just as it hit the porch, his hand grasping one of the thick black straps, then tightening, indicating his unease.

The brand name on the backpack was one Jake recognized, which made him realize that the boy wasn't just some displaced kid off the streets. He belonged to somebody, Jake thought, immediately alarmed.

"You're Jacob Matthew McCall, aren't you?" the boy asked. His gaze held Jake's, and though his voice held determination, his shoulders slumped a bit in defeat.

Jake nodded and waited. It seemed like forever before the boy spoke again.

"I came a long way to meet you," he stated, his green eyes cautious, as if he wasn't sure of his welcome or what to expect from his sudden visit.

Jake was sorry to see so little trust in such a young boy's eyes. Who was he, and where had he come from?

When he had answered the door and seen the boy, he'd thought he had come from the nearby town of Crockett. School had just let out for the year, and several kids had stopped by to ask for summer work—mostly teenagers who lived in town and had never set foot on a ranch.

The boy said he'd come a long way. Jake looked

behind him, but didn't see a car. "How'd you get here?" he asked.

The youngster's lips curved into the bare resemblance of a smile. "I took a bus, then hitched a couple of rides. I got a ride in Ozona with someone who was headed for Crockett. I was walking this way when a lady stopped her car and waved me over. She said her ranch was next to yours, and she gave me a lift here."

"Mary Beth Adams?" Jake asked, thinking of his neighbor.

"Yeah, that was her name," the kid replied as he nodded his head.

Jake couldn't believe this young boy had taken such risks. That aside, the secrecy of the boy's parentage must have been burning in his heart to have made him take drastic chances.

Jake knew firsthand how secrets could drive a person crazy. When he'd taken over the ranch after his parents' death, he'd learned that the woman he'd known and loved as his mother hadn't given birth to him. He'd never been able to discuss it with anyone, not even his brothers or sister. Jake shook the hurtful thoughts from his mind. This wasn't about him or the family secret he'd buried in his heart.

He looked again at the boy whose green eyes were watching him. It took a lot of guts for the kid to knock on Jake's door and confront him. Jake knew his size intimidated most people. At six-two, he towered over most men, given the exception of his brother Ryder, who was six-three. Their younger brother, Deke, wasn't far behind them at six foot. The fact that Jake was the least outgoing of the bunch sometimes made him seem unapproachable to strangers, yet this kid had faced Jake without hesitation.

The boy shrugged. "She said you go by 'Jake' and described what you look like, so I figured I had the right person when you answered the door."

"What's your name?" Jake asked, studying the boy while trying to figure out where he'd gotten such an absurd notion. Oddly, he did look a tad familiar. There was something about the color of his deep-green eyes that tugged at Jake's memory.

He wished he knew why. At thirty-four, Jake wasn't ancient by any means, so at least his mind wasn't slipping. Maybe it was that he had a bit too much to think about lately. Ryder and Ashley, his wife, had brought twin daughters into their family home, which added a new, but welcome, dimension to all of their lives.

Jake quelled the flash of envy that sometimes attacked him when he thought of his two baby nieces, and reminded himself that he was happy for his brother.

"Matthew. My friends call me Matt," he answered, his expression guarded. As if gathering courage, he straightened and his shoulders stiffened.

Noticing that Matt didn't offer his full name, Jake didn't know what to make of the kid. A strange, not at all comfortable feeling crawled up Jake's spine. Odd that they shared the same name, though Matthew was Jake's middle name and he'd never gone by it. Jake tossed that off as pure coincidence and probably one of the reasons the kid had mistakenly knocked on Jake's door.

The one thing in his life that Jake was positive about was that there was no way he'd fathered a child. Not long after he'd returned to the ranch, Jake had been thrown from a horse he'd been training. In a fury the horse had stomped on him and left Jake unable to have children. He had been devastated when the doctor had told him, but in time he'd learned to accept it.

It wasn't until he'd met and dated Maxine that Jake realized not having children meant he would never get married. He and Maxine had been seeing each other for nearly six months when Jake had confessed he was unable to father a child. She'd been upset, but she'd told him she loved him, that it didn't make a difference.

Foolishly Jake had believed her. He'd started making plans to ask her to marry him. He'd even bought her a ring. His heart cramped with renewed pain of the memory. The night he was going to propose she'd abruptly broken off their relationship, telling him she'd thought she could live with his "condition," was what she called it, but she'd changed her mind. She wanted a *whole* man.

Hurt and disillusioned, Jake had vowed never to allow himself to be that vulnerable to a woman again. He didn't need a permanent relationship in his life. He settled for an occasional evening or two of pleasure when he desired company.

Still, it was painful when he thought about never being a father, especially when Ryder seemed intent on populating the entire county singlehandedly. With the twins, Michelle and Melissa, and another baby on the way, Ryder was walking around with a silly grin on his face nearly all the time.

Jake glanced over the boy once again, taking note that his head came to about Jake's chest. His size, Jake thought, was deceiving. Hazarding a guess, Jake figured he was around twelve, much too young to be traveling alone.

"Well, Matt," Jake began, opening the screened

door to the porch, "why don't you come inside, and let's see if we can figure this thing out."

Matt hoisted his backpack onto his shoulder. He stepped inside the house, and his gaze darted around the large foyer, taking in his surroundings with wide-open eyes.

Jake closed the door, and silence filled the air between them. He wasn't quite sure what to do next. He knew he had to get a handle on this mix-up quickly. The kid's family was sure to be worried about him. Before Jake could say anything, Ryder came around the corner from the hall that led to the dining room.

"Ashley sent me to find you. The babies have been fed, and we don't have much quiet time. She said she's not going to hold dinner much longer, that you'd better get your butt in there." Ryder was smiling, but then he noticed the young boy standing by the front door. He stopped abruptly and flashed a curious glance at Jake.

"This is Matt," Jake said by way of an introduction. "Matt, this is my brother, Ryder." Ryder stuck out his hand, and the boy shook it.

"You come by looking for a job?" Ryder asked, taking another look at the kid, then watching his brother.

"Not exactly," Jake answered for the boy. "It seems we have some business to discuss. Go ahead and eat. I'll be in, in a little while." Ryder's curious gaze flickered from Jake to Matt, but he left without commenting.

"Let's go somewhere more private to talk," Jake said, then indicated for Matt to follow him down a hallway. Once inside the large ranch office, Jake extended his hand toward a brown vinyl sofa.

"Have a seat," he told Matt, then walked over to a large walnut desk and leaned his rear against it, bracing his hands against the edge. His gaze followed Matt as he sat down.

"Now, just to be up-front with you, I have to tell you I'm positive I'm not who you're looking for, but why don't you start at the beginning. Where are you from?" he asked, crossing his arms and staring at the youth.

"Lubbock."

Jake nodded and his brows wrinkled. "I went to school there for a while."

"I know."

The two words once again robbed Jake of breath. Jake was stunned by Matt's answer. How much did this kid know about him, and how did he find it out? "You do, huh?"

"Yes, sir." Matt's gaze never left Jake. "You went to Texas Tech, right?"

Jake's eyes widened so slightly it was barely noticeable. He'd attended Texas Tech until his parents were killed. Then he'd returned home to take care of his siblings.

Jake figured that although it was out of the ordinary for Mary Beth to gossip, she must have been the one to mention such information to Matt. Of course, it could have been anyone who lived around Crockett.

Everyone within a hundred miles of their ranch and the town knew Jake and his family. And most of those people knew that he hadn't finished school, that he'd left to come home and take over his parents' ranch when they died in an airplane crash. And that he'd raised his younger siblings. Still, Jake didn't think Matt had come into contact with anyone other than Mary Beth.

Matt was sitting on the edge of his seat. "I found a paper that my mom had in a chest in her bedroom. That's how I found out that you're my father."

Jake felt a little pang every time the boy called him his father. He couldn't deny the yearning and disappointment that pulled at him. A little part of Jake's heart twisted, wishing for something that was unattainable.

He supposed most people would think that after raising three siblings, he'd pretty much raised a family. Jake had told himself that same thing many times and wished he felt that way in his heart. He had been responsible for his brothers and his sister, Lynn, since he was twenty-one, but had never felt that they were a substitute for having a family of his own. Maybe that's why it had been so hard to watch each of them grow and mature. He had nothing to take their place.

It wasn't until Ryder had become a father that Jake realized how much he would miss by not having children. While he was happy for Ryder and Ashley, a little twinge of jealousy simmered in Jake's heart. Ironically, Ryder had been the one who hadn't wanted children, but he'd found the love of his life and had settled down and started raising a family.

Jake knew he would never be able to do the same.

"What kind of paper?" he asked, bringing his thoughts back to the problem at hand. The kid was staring at him as if he had the power to fulfill his dreams.

"A hospital paper."

"Like a certificate—the kind with your footprints?" Matt nodded, but gave nothing more away.

Jake's lips thinned as he thought about it. "Do you have it with you?"

Matt lifted his pack onto his lap and zipped open an outside pocket. He searched through it for a few moments, then produced a folded piece of paper and handed it to Jake. "It has your address written on it."

As Matt said, Jake's address was written on the back side. For some reason the handwriting looked familiar. Sighing, he opened it and studied what looked like a legitimate hospital certificate, the folded creases worn.

The first thing that Jake searched for was his name on the document. A jolt went through him when he saw it printed neatly beside the word *father*. It was a natural response to look immediately at the line listing the mother's name, and Jake's heart took another blow when he actually recognized it.

Catherine St. John.

Jake's hand shook as he stared at the paper, and he was unprepared for the rush of emotions that assailed him. His chest squeezed painfully. He couldn't seem to get a handle on something as basic as breathing and hated feeling so out of control.

All of his life he'd been the one to shoulder responsibilities, to make decisions, to carry them out and make sure that the ranch ran smoothly and his siblings were well cared for.

How long had it been since he'd thought of Catie? he wondered, letting his mind slide back to his college years. He'd met her at school, had fallen in love with her. They'd even talked about marriage. But they both knew there was school to finish, and Catie's father would have had a fit if he'd known how involved they were.

Catie.

Her face drifted through his thoughts. A beautiful brunette, tall and lithe, she'd touched his soul. But Jake had let go of her and their promise of a future together.

He remembered that the last time he'd seen her, they'd had a fight over something. What about, he couldn't even remember now. That night he'd gotten the call about his parents, and he'd returned home to deal with the responsibilities at the ranch and to care for his siblings.

And somewhere along the way, he'd lost Catie. Jake stared at Matt. This was Catie's son.

His Catie.

No, he corrected himself harshly, not *his* Catie. He'd given up the right to call Catie his a long time ago. He was ashamed that he'd never called her, but he'd arrived home to find the ranch deep in debt, and it had taken all of his time and energy for a while to keep it afloat. Then, there was the accident. In all fairness, Jake told himself, Catie hadn't called him, either.

Jake looked up to find Matt watching him. He took a deep breath and strove to get his emotions under control.

"Catie St. John is your mother?" he asked, and his voice took on a new huskiness. He cleared his throat, willing away the tightness inside his chest, the grip of emotion that seized him. Instead, it became worse, carving at him like the sharpened blade of a knife.

Matt nodded a little hesitantly. "I've never heard anyone call her Catie," he answered. "She goes by Catherine."

Jake digested that information. He'd shortened her name to Catie shortly after they'd met.

"Matt, did your mother *tell* you I was your father?" There had to be some mistake, some reason Catie had listed his name on her son's certificate. Though it was only seconds, it seemed as if an eternity passed before Matt finally answered.

"No," he admitted, then glanced away momentarily. "I didn't really ask her."

"You didn't ask her?" Jake repeated. Lines indented the skin between his brows as he stared at Matt. "You mean you didn't talk to her about this?" His tone was incredulous.

Matt's head moved from side to side.

"Are you telling me that Catie—your mother," he amended, "doesn't even know that you were curious about your father?" he asked roughly, astonished that the boy wouldn't have discussed something this important with his mother before he took off on his own. What kind of relationship did they share? Had the sweet young woman he'd known changed so much? Was she that unapproachable?

"She doesn't have time for me anymore," Matt stated, a little defiance in his tone. "She's getting married soon. I thought if I found my father, that maybe…maybe I could live with him for a while. I don't have that long until I graduate and then I can be on my own." For the first time he looked worried, as if his plan had flaws that he hadn't even thought about.

Jake laid the paper on the desk, then straightened his shoulders and crossed his arms in front of him. The news that Catie was about to get married shouldn't have bothered him, but his gut tightened a fraction. "Don't you think she might be worried about you?"

Guilt flashed through Matt's eyes. "I guess so," he admitted. His Adam's apple bobbed as he swallowed hard. A sadness stole over his young features. He seemed to want so much to appear grown-up, but Jake saw only a young boy with a need for attention, a need for a father. "I guess you didn't want anything to do with me." He looked right at Jake, staring at him as if his very life depended on his answer.

Jake swore, then murmured an apology to the boy. Jake had let his father's lawyer, Frank Davis, handle all of the correspondence for the ranch. Surely he would have passed any personal letters on to Jake.

"Believe me, Matt, if I'd known about you, I damn sure would have contacted your mother." He stood and paced to the window, looking out at the expanse of the Bar M, his family's ranch. He'd given his life to keep the ranch going, to make sure his family stayed together. Had he given up his son, too?

Turning, he stared at the boy. Yes, now he could see Catie in him and knew that was why Matt had looked so familiar when he'd come to the door. His nose was just like hers and there was something about the way he tilted his head when he talked. Catie used to do that.

Matt was watching him, so Jake walked back over to within a couple of feet of him. "I have to tell you, Matt, that I still believe there's some mistake, but I think we'd better call your mother right away. I'm sure she's very worried about you."

Matt stood, and his stance became rigid. "I don't want to go back to live with her. Can't I stay here? I won't be any trouble, I swear. I do pretty good in school, and I can be a real help on your ranch."

Jake's heart filled with compassion, but he didn't let himself believe that Matt was his son. Jake was sure Catie would provide a reasonable explanation once he got in touch with her.

"I can't make you any promises, Matt. The first thing we have to do is talk to your mother."

Matt looked scared and uneasy. Jake lifted the receiver of the telephone and extended it toward him. When he didn't move immediately to grasp it, Jake shook it gently, encouraging the boy to take it.

Matt put the receiver to his ear. Leaning over the desk, he punched some numbers in, then cast a guarded look at Jake as he waited for it to ring. Moments later his eyes darkened when his mother answered.

"Hey, Mom. It's me, Matt."

Silence stretched as Matt listened to his mother's response. Jake wished now that he'd put the phone on speaker so he could hear what Catie was saying. He was surprised at his anticipation of talking to her, even under these strange and unexpected circumstances.

Matt said, "I'm okay, Mom. I'm sorry I scared you." For a couple of minutes more Matt just listened. Jake watched as the boy turned away to hide the tears in his eyes. "I know, Mom. I'm sorry. I really am." His voice shook enough to betray his emotions, and he took a deep breath.

"I know you're going to be mad, but I came to see my father," Matt whispered into the receiver. "I found the hospital paper with his address. You know, the one in the chest in your room."

Jake watched the boy talk. He was genuinely remorseful, and Jake was impressed. Matt had manners and a conscience, and it seemed as if Catie had raised her son well.

Their son.

Jake's mind wandered automatically. Could it be true? Was Matt his son? He looked again at the boy for some sort of physical sign. Besides his height, all he could see was Catie. Matt had her brown hair color, her dark-green eyes.

Matt couldn't be his son, Jake told himself again. There was no way Catie wouldn't have let him know he'd fathered a child. She wouldn't have kept Matt to herself for all these years. Jake was drawn from his thoughts when Matt held the receiver out to him.

"My mom wants to speak to you," he said, sounding every bit as contrite as he looked.

Jake hesitated a moment before grasping the telephone, taking a breath to prepare himself. Finally he raised the phone to his ear.

"Catie, this is Jake."

There was a long silence on the line, and for a moment or two, Jake thought he'd lost the connection. Then she spoke.

"Jake."

Hearing her say his name touched a vast emptiness inside him. Her voice nearly crumbled, and Jake felt her pain. She must have been out of her mind with worry when she discovered Matt was missing.

"How are you, Catie?" Jake made himself say the words. Emotion choked him, making him feel as if he was locked in a box and suffocating.

"Fine. I'm fine. And it's Catherine," she added, her tone containing none of the warmth that Jake remembered from when they were together. "Look, I'm sorry about this." Again, she faltered, unable, it seemed, to go on.

"He's all right, Catherine." Her name sounded foreign to him even as he said it. He felt as if he was in some kind of time warp.

Through the telephone, Jake could sense Catherine's terror. She sounded desperate and exhausted. He looked at Matt and, for a moment, wanted to strangle the kid. What had he been thinking to run off without talking to his mother?

After an audible gasp of breath, she spoke again. "I was so worried. I was afraid that something terrible had happened to Matthew. So many bad things can happen to children today. I don't know what got into him."

"He looks a bit tired, but other than that he's okay. Don't worry about him."

"Thank you for calling me," Catherine whispered through the line.

Jake hesitated, then replied, "It was no problem." Their conversation was stilted, filled with an awkwardness of years gone by, which left Jake wondering how much Catie had changed. When they were together, they'd been able to talk about anything. Now it was as if they were strangers.

Well, they were, he reminded himself. He didn't know this Catherine, and she knew nothing about him. They weren't the same two kids who fell in love in college.

"How on earth did Matthew get there?"

"He said he caught a bus, then hitched a couple of rides," Jake told her, repeating what Matt had told him.

"Oh, my— Jake, I'm leaving right away to come and get him."

Jake glanced at his watch and frowned. "It's late. Why don't you wait until morning?" he suggested, thinking it wouldn't be a good idea for her to travel while she was so upset. Then he thought it ridiculous that he was concerned about her. She probably wouldn't be traveling alone.

"I'm coming right now, Jake." Catherine's voice held a you-can't-stop-me tone and Jake shuddered. He knew she was worried, but for some reason he thought there was more to it than that. Jake heard the panic in her voice and glanced at Matt who was across the room, leaning against a wall. He looked scared, uneasy and worried.

"Hold on a minute," Jake said into the receiver, then placed his hand over the mouthpiece. "Matt, why don't you wait in the family room while I talk to your mother?" he suggested. "It's the second room as you go out." Matt didn't move and Jake added, "Go on."

After a moment's hesitation, Matt nodded.

Jake waited while Matt went out the door, then put the receiver back to his ear. "I've sent Matt out of the room so we can talk in private," he informed Catherine.

"That really wasn't necessary. The only thing I have to say is that I'm coming to get him. Right now." Her tone was curt, determined.

"Catie, wait." Jake realized he'd reverted to his nickname for her. He frowned, and the thought occurred to him that some habits never change.

He had hoped to wait until he saw her in person, when he could better judge what she was telling him by her expression. But he needed to know the truth. It seemed as if she wanted to come and whisk Matt away without any explanation. Jake wasn't going to let that happen.

He wanted answers.

"Catie, Matt told me why he came here," Jake stated, and the bald statement created a tense strain of silence on the line.

"What...what exactly did he say, Jake?" she asked, her voice once again unsteady.

"He showed me a hospital certificate with my name

on it.'' He let that sit between them for a moment, wanting her to absorb the shock as he'd had to.

When she didn't say anything, Jake took a deep breath. It took every ounce of his courage to ask the question on his mind. ''Is it true, Catie? Am I Matt's father?''

Two

Catherine St. John grasped the telephone receiver tighter, holding on to it like a drowning person would cling to a life preserver after a shipwreck at sea. Her heart stopped, and she squeezed her eyes closed.

Am I Matt's father?

She had been dreading that question for much longer than Jake McCall could possibly imagine. For thirteen years, since the day she'd learned she was pregnant, she'd wondered when this day would come. She'd thought about it, worried about it, feared it. There was rarely a day when she didn't think about Jake or the circumstances that left her pregnant and alone.

"Jake—" Her pleading tone implied stalling and Jake cut her off.

"Catie, I want the truth. *Now. Is Matt my son?*" Jake demanded.

"Yes."

The whispered word was barely audible. The immediate silence it brought was deafening.

Jake was the one who broke it, and his tone wasn't kind. "Why, Catie?" he demanded, sounding incredulous, angry and not at all understanding. "Why in hell didn't you ever tell me?"

Catherine's first thought was to try again to put the conversation off. She was already dealing with one crisis—she couldn't handle another. Not now. Not when she'd been sick with worry for hours, wondering where Matthew was and whether or not he was safe.

"I don't think we should be discussing this over the telephone," she answered quickly, hoping she didn't sound as panicked as she felt. She needed time to think, time to pull herself together. "I'm leaving to come there shortly. We can discuss it then." Her suggestion was met with silence, and she added, "I'll be there as soon as possible."

"Matt's exhausted and probably hungry. I'm sure he can use a night's sleep. You can come in the morning," Jake told her. "Get a flight to San Luis, then rent a car. You could probably be here by early afternoon."

"I want to come now," she insisted, her voice rising just a notch.

"He's not going anywhere, and it seems to me that you both need a few hours to get yourselves together. I'll see to it that he doesn't leave here," Jake promised.

"I'm not concerned with him leaving again."

"Then what are you concerned about?"

Catherine sighed heavily. "Jake, it's complicated. Matt should never have come to you. He's mixed up right now."

"Catie—"

"He's *my* son. I'm sorry that you were brought into

this, that he came all the way there before I had a chance to clear things up with him. But I'm not letting him stay any longer than necessary.''

After a moment Jake surprised her by agreeing. ''You're right,'' he replied. ''We should discuss this in person.'' Then his voice lowered to a deep, determined tone. ''Tomorrow.''

''I don't want to wait until tomorrow,'' Catherine declared, and her voice cracked a bit. If she waited until morning, it would be afternoon before she got there. She put a hand to her temple and massaged the headache that had started the moment she had heard Jake McCall's voice.

''I'm not giving you a choice.'' Jake's tone was sharp and to the point. It left little room for arguing.

''That's not—''

''What? Fair? Is that what you were going to say?'' he demanded, cutting her off once again.

''Jake—''

''Look,'' he said roughly as he argued the point. ''Matt's upset. It might be best to give him some time to work things out. You can just as easily fly in tomorrow.''

Catie stiffened and grasped the telephone tighter, her knuckles turning white. She tried very hard to stay calm, but Jake was making it terribly difficult.

''I don't need you to tell me what's best for my son.'' How could Jake even know what was best for Matthew? He hadn't even known the boy existed until today.

''Apparently you do,'' Jake countered. ''He ran away from you. That tells me he wasn't happy.''

Catherine bristled, and the anger she'd held in check

until now began to seep out. "It wasn't like that. You don't know anything about him, Jake."

Jake's voice took on a hard edge. "You're wrong, Catie. I know one thing for damn sure. I know now that he's my son."

Catherine hung up the receiver. In the end she'd given in and agreed to arrive at Jake's ranch tomorrow. Under the circumstances it seemed the best way to handle the entire situation.

And it wasn't as if Jake had given her a choice. Oh, she could ignore him and leave immediately. But Jake had already begun sounding hostile, and Catherine didn't want to make an enemy of Jake McCall. Not now. Not while Matthew was in Jake's home.

Catherine went to her room and began packing a bag of clothes. After throwing in the necessary items for a day's stay, she walked to Matthew's room and retrieved a change of clothing for her son and put them in with her things.

Why hadn't she seen this coming? she wondered. Had she been so out of tune to Matthew's needs that she'd missed warning signals that something was terribly wrong in her son's life?

She'd noticed that he'd been distant and moody over the past few months, but Catherine had just tossed that up to his being an adolescent. All adolescents went through personality changes. As a high school counselor, she knew that well enough. Catherine hadn't thought there was anything to worry about. Matthew was a good kid. He was respectful and made decent grades. She'd thought that he just needed some time, that he'd come around.

But she'd been wrong. So terribly wrong.

Though Matthew had known about the chest in her

room, she hadn't thought that he'd go into it on his own. She remembered when he was about eight and had come upon Catherine going through some of the contents. When he'd seen a picture of her and Jake together, he'd asked if the man was his father. Catherine had told him the truth, that his father was someone she'd known in college. Matthew hadn't asked about his father since that day.

What had she ever done to make her son feel as if she didn't want him around? Since his birth there had just been the two of them. When Catherine had found out she was pregnant, Jake had already left college and returned home to take care of his younger brothers and sister. Catherine had tried to call him. She'd left a couple of messages, but Jake had never returned her calls.

They'd argued the night before he'd left. Jake's roommate had told her of Jake's parents' death. She'd wanted to go to him, but her father hadn't permitted her to. When weeks passed with no word from him, Catherine had been hurt, assuming that he'd meant to break off their relationship.

Only when she learned she was pregnant did Catherine decide to write him and ask him to contact her. Instead of getting a letter from Jake, she'd received one from his lawyer stating that Jake didn't know her. It was then that she'd decided not to tell him about the baby. She loved him, but she didn't want Jake back because she was pregnant with his child. She'd wanted his love, but he'd shut her out of his life.

Leaning over the table, Catherine held her head against her palms and closed her eyes. She'd felt betrayed and hurt, and she'd held on to that anger for years. It had provided her with the will to take care of herself and her baby. She'd fed on it every time things got rough and she felt like giving up.

How she'd even gotten through the first few weeks after finding out she was pregnant was a blur. She had wanted to stay in school, but without help it was impossible. In desperation, Catherine had turned to her family.

Reverend St. John, her father, had been a rigid disciplinarian. Catherine had feared the fire-and-brimstone preacher for most of her life, so she hadn't expected him to be pleased when she told him of her predicament. She'd known her parents would be upset when they learned of her pregnancy, but she had relied on at least getting some moral support. She had never considered that they would disown her.

Her father had given her a cold, distant stare, then informed Catherine that she was a disgrace to her family. Catherine's mother had watched and said nothing as he belittled his daughter. Her mother had always bowed to her husband's authority, and Catherine couldn't remember one time when her mother had stood up to him.

Catherine cringed as her past came rushing back at her. The hurtful memories caused tears to spring to her eyes. Her father had called her some unforgivable names. That she still felt the pain, after all this time, angered her. She hadn't even been allowed to stay in touch with her two younger sisters. That had hurt the most.

Get yourself together, she mentally admonished herself. She had made it through all of that. She had gotten a job to support herself and had finished college while taking care of a small child. She'd eventually received her master's degree and was working at a rewarding career, was able to provide well for Matthew and herself.

Catherine had been through hell and back, and she was stronger for it. She wasn't going to let Jake McCall bully her. If he thought she was going to roll over and play dead, he was wrong. Catherine St. John was a fighter. Jake McCall had himself to thank for that.

Early the next morning Catherine put her bag in the passenger side of her car. She hesitated only a moment before walking around and getting behind the wheel.

She'd called Douglas last night to tell him that she'd found Matthew. She and Douglas Anders had been dating for a while, long enough to talk about marriage, and Catherine had wanted him to know that Matthew was safe.

He'd been supportive when she had called, had even offered to drive her to the airport, then only seconds later mentioned that he'd have to rearrange an important meeting. Catherine had felt that the offer hadn't really been sincere, but she'd shrugged it off. She was used to Douglas putting his work first.

She'd admired his dedication to his job when she'd first met him and now reminded herself that his job as a stockbroker was demanding. He was a dependable man, someone steady in her life after being alone for so long.

She had told Douglas that she'd probably be back by late evening, and now she hoped it wasn't wishful thinking. She wasn't leaving Matthew at Jake's, no matter what it took. Her son was coming home with her.

Catherine started the engine, then backed out of the driveway. She switched on the air conditioner as she started toward the airport. Since it was early in the morning, the car began to cool instantly. However, it did little to relieve the anxiety Catherine felt building inside her. The last thing she wanted to do was to face Jake after all these years, after all the heartache he'd given her.

She pushed her hand through her hair, brushing it off her shoulder and behind her back. The memories came rushing back at her as if only days had passed instead of thirteen years.

Jake McCall had been her first and only true love. Her father had never allowed her a boyfriend while she was living at home, so she'd had little experience when it came to boys. She hadn't been prepared for her reaction to Jake when she met him. She'd known soon after she met Jake that she had lost her heart to him.

She'd first seen him during her second semester of college. He'd been a couple of years older, and there was something about Jake McCall that attracted her attention. In fact, he drew a lot of attention from girls. He was tall and there was a certain ruggedness about him. She'd heard that he was from a ranching family, which was evident by his muscular arms and trim body. With dark-brown hair and brown eyes, he was rogue handsome.

He'd been so serious about school, not into partying like a lot of the other kids. Even from afar, before she'd even met Jake, Catherine had admired that about him.

She'd never dreamed that Jake McCall would take a second look at her. But he'd approached her after one of her classes, and they'd spent the afternoon walking in a park and chatting. Later they'd gone to a restaurant and talked away the night. They had seen each other every day after that, neither of them wanting to be with anyone else. The more she was with Jake, the more Catherine wanted to be with him.

Trying to shake memories of Jake from her mind, Catherine switched on the radio as she headed down the interstate toward the airport. She'd called and arranged a flight as soon as she'd hung up with Jake last night, then she'd called him back to let him know when to expect her.

After parking her car in the long-term lot, Catherine made her way to the ticket area, then proceeded to the departure gate. She'd timed her arrival well and only had to wait about fifteen minutes before the airline attendant called her flight.

A mixture of relief and trepidation filled Catherine when she arrived in San Luis. All she could think about was driving as fast as she could to Jake's ranch. Though she told herself that she had nothing to worry about, she felt like a bucket of nerves as she stood waiting for her turn to leave her seat.

Catherine retrieved her bag from the overhead compartment and followed the trail of people ahead of her off the airplane, mentally calculating the time it would take to make the drive ahead of her. She'd gotten the directions from Jake earlier and hoped she wouldn't get lost. From what Jake said, it wouldn't take terribly long.

Upon entering the terminal, Catherine's eyes were drawn to the big man leaning nonchalantly against the wall across the small walkway. She started to look past him, then her gaze was pulled back to him of its own will. Her heart shifted and a chill ran down her spine. He had on a black cowboy hat and snug blue jeans that hugged his hips. Small drops of water dripped from his Stetson and dotted his white cotton shirt.

Jake.

As soon as Catherine recognized him, she stopped dead in her tracks. Someone bumped into her, and she barely caught herself, then stepped aside. When she looked up, the full force of Jake's attention staggered her. A freight train would have caused less of an impact.

Jake's gaze traveled lazily over her, from her head to her toes, then back up to her face. He never for one moment gave her a hint of what he was thinking. Catherine wished she looked as calm, but she knew better. She was trembling all over. Surely he could tell.

Catherine still hadn't moved when Jake easily shifted his weight away from the wall and moved toward her. She stood frozen, unable to do anything but watch him slowly make his way in her direction. He stopped in front of her, and she immediately resented the fact that his mere presence robbed her of the ability to breathe.

His granite expression startled her, as did the distant look in his dark-brown eyes—eyes that she remembered being warm and loving. It shocked her to see that he'd changed so much.

He stared at her silently for more than a moment, then tipped his hat up just a bit, leaving his face slightly shadowed.

''Catherine.''

On the trip out to pick her up, Jake had worked on how to respond to seeing Catherine after all this time. He told himself to use her given name when referring to her and, as silly as it sounded, he'd even practiced doing so. Anger wasn't something he usually had to work at defusing. Unlike his brother Ryder, Jake wasn't prone to flying off the handle. It took a lot to provoke him.

But, dammit, he was angry with Catherine for keeping his son from him, and he would use any means at his disposal to keep his guard up. He wasn't going to go easy on her now. He had to admit that he was tempted, seeing that she looked scared and overwrought. It would have been easy to comfort her, to tell her everything would be all right.

But Jake couldn't do that. He couldn't be nice to her. He had to keep that edge. His future with his son was at stake, and he wasn't going to give Catherine any leverage over him.

What Catherine had done had basically ruined his easygoing reputation. Ryder and Ashley had tried to get Jake to calm down and give Catherine a chance to explain why she'd kept his son a secret from him.

But secrets could tear a family apart. Jake found that out when he'd taken over the ranch. And he'd kept his father's infidelity a secret to himself, rather than see his brothers and sister hurt. He'd never discussed what he knew with them, even when Ryder had kept insisting that there had to be a good reason for Catherine to keep Matthew a secret from Jake.

In the end Jake had agreed to give Catherine a chance to explain why she hadn't told him about his son, why she had let Jake miss seeing Matthew grow up.

That was before he'd seen her walk off the airplane. Then the anger and frustration settled deeper in his soul.

Jake was pleased that he'd managed not to convey any of the emotions boiling around inside him. He was honest enough to admit to himself that a part of him had been looking forward to seeing Catherine again, but he hadn't *wanted* to feel that way, and he resented the fact that he did.

He wasn't prepared for the sight of her. Dressed in designer jeans and a soft pink shirt, she was still slim, though her body was more womanly, filled out nicely in all the right places. Her hips were gently rounded, her face a bit fuller. She wore her hair shorter, just below her shoulders, its color a rich chocolate-brown. Her features were soft and inviting, her lips sculpted perfectly.

Her breasts, well, damn, Jake thought, they'd filled out as well, and he couldn't stop his gaze from resting on them a moment longer than necessary. Catherine had never been small. Jake could remember how firm her breasts had been when he'd last touched them and found himself wondering how they would feel now.

Before he let himself go farther down that road, he hauled his wayward thoughts back. Jake didn't like the way his body immediately responded to Catherine. The last thing he wanted was to feel any kind of attraction to her. That was dangerous territory, and he knew he had to steer clear of it if he was going to keep his mind sharp. Something told him he'd need every ounce of his mental faculties when dealing with her.

Three

Though last night Catherine had wanted Jake to use her full name, she was taken aback by the aloofness of his tone. The way he said it made her shiver with apprehension. She stared at him and swallowed past the lump in her throat. Tears stung her eyes as she thought of the gentle, loving young man she'd known so many years ago. There was no trace of him in the hard, distant person standing before her.

"Jake," she whispered, an ache in her heart appearing out of nowhere. There was disappointment and sadness in her voice. Too many years had passed since she'd seen Jake. There was so much she wanted to say, so much she wanted to know. She wanted to ask about broken promises, wanted to know why he had discarded her love and broken her heart.

"What...what are you doing here?" was all she managed to get out, and she decided that she should be thankful that she sounded remotely normal. "I thought I told you that I was renting a car. I'd planned on driving out to get Matthew."

"You did," he acknowledged, his clipped tone cutting her no slack. He hooked his arms together across his chest.

Catherine was having a bit of trouble following their conversation. "Then why are you here?" she asked again. Her brows wrinkled.

"I decided to save you the trouble."

He reached toward her, and Catherine braced herself for his touch. Her heart skipped several beats. Jake took her bag from her and easily lifted it. A shock of disappointment rocked through her.

Well, what had she expected? He wasn't likely to embrace her, now, was he? And it was ridiculous for her to even entertain such a notion.

But the memories that had assailed her last night had continued to this very moment. Catherine had wondered if Jake would look anything the way she remembered. While she'd recognized him instantly, there was little about him that reminded her of the young man she'd once loved with all her heart and innocence.

"That isn't necessary." As if he hadn't understood her plans, she explained once again. "I've already made arrangements to rent a car. I'd like to get on the road back to Lubbock as soon as possible." She waited for him to acknowledge her words, but he remained quiet, his gaze boring into her. "I told you that, on the telephone last night," she reminded him when he continued to stare at her without speaking.

Catherine looked at his face and decided the years had been good to Jake. Too good. Though tiny lines creased the corners of his brown eyes and bracketed his mouth, his face was lean and tanned. Irritation swept through her. She would have preferred him to be balding and fat.

Not a chance. Apparently, years of working on his ranch had perfected his physique, giving him muscles and a rock-hard body that Douglas spent hours in a health club trying to achieve.

"I thought if I picked you up we could discuss the situation on the way to the ranch," he said, then nodded his head. "This way." He stood aside and waited.

Catherine didn't move. The last thing she wanted was to give Jake the idea that they were going to discuss what was best for Matthew. It wasn't up for debate. "I'm here to get my son. He should never have come here."

Jake's gaze swung back at her, and his eyes met hers with deadly force. "You're wrong about that," he replied, his tone unnervingly calm. "Matt is my son. *Mine*. And he has every right to be here."

It took every ounce of her courage for Catherine to hold her ground and not back away from Jake. "You don't even know him, Jake," she declared defensively.

Jake's expression turned colder. "And whose fault is that?" he demanded. When Catherine didn't answer, he said, "Look, we can have this out right here for all of San Luis to see, or we can talk in private. It's up to you. Right now I don't really give a damn. But I'll warn you that my temper is at a boiling point. You can continue to push me if you want, but you might not like the end result."

He stared at her, his expression unforgiving, and Catherine thought his heart would be just as hard to reach. If she was going to make any ground with Jake, she was going to have to work for it.

It was in her favor to at least be civil with him. She didn't want a fight for her son on her hands. She wanted her son plain and simple. She was going to do whatever she had to do to bring Matthew back home where he belonged.

Catherine had a bad feeling that no matter what she said, Jake wasn't going to like it. Still she didn't want to let him get the upper hand. "I don't know," she said, looking around them and realizing that they were drawing the attention of some of the people in the small airport. "I prefer to have my own transportation."

She started walking away from him but knew without looking behind her that Jake was following. When they neared the desk for the rental agency, she heard him call her name.

Catherine stopped and swung back toward him. For a brief moment he sounded like the young man she'd once known and loved, and the years dropped away as if they'd never happened. Yet, all she had to do was to meet his intense gaze and she realized again how much he had changed.

There was a hard edge to him now that hadn't been there years ago. His demeanor was remote, his eyes distrustful. Catherine's heart softened. What had his life been like? she wondered.

Catherine immediately put a damper on those thoughts. She couldn't afford to let down her guard where Jake was concerned.

"You really don't need a car. I'll bring you back as soon as you're ready to leave."

He looked as if he meant it, but Catherine was still filled with apprehension. She didn't know Jake now. He was nothing like the young man she'd fallen in love with. He'd hurt her once before. Nothing had changed. She had no reason to trust him.

Maybe he's thinking the same thing about you.

The thought jarred her. Was that what Jake was thinking about her? That she couldn't be trusted? Did she even care? After she retrieved her son, there would be no more contact between her and Jake. Perhaps the best thing was for them both to start over. Maybe she should make the first effort by accepting his offer to drive her, she thought. After all, he *had* made the trip to pick her up. The least she could do was to accept graciously.

"I'll ride to your ranch to pick up Matthew if you promise to bring me back to the airport without an argument," she stated, then waited for his reply.

Jake hesitated a moment, then nodded. "You have my word."

Catherine wanted to believe Jake. She told herself that she had nothing to worry about. The ride from San Luis to Crockett, where Jake's ranch was located, wouldn't take that long. She could stand being alone with him for the time it would take to pick up her son. The quick return trip to the airport would be worth it. With luck she and Matthew would be home before midnight.

As they stepped outside they were showered with pellets of water. It was a heavy downpour, and wind and rain whipped at their faces.

"Wait inside," Jake instructed, then pushed her back through the door.

Catherine watched him make his way to a white Suburban. He tossed her bag in the back, then got in behind the wheel. A minute later he pulled up to the curb. Before she'd gotten out of the door, he was at her side and ushering her to the truck, blocking as much of the rain as he could with his big body.

Catherine was relieved when he closed the door behind her. She hadn't had time to think about having Jake so close to her, and she didn't like the way her heart hammered when he'd touched her back.

He slipped behind the wheel before she had a chance to take a deep breath. His nearness was having an unwelcome effect on her body. Catherine hoped the ride wouldn't take long. When she'd agreed to let him drive her, she hadn't thought about being alone in such close quarters.

He turned the key, and the engine roared to life. With deft movements he pulled out of his parking spot and they left the airport in silence.

"Whew," Catherine sighed, running her fingers through her damp hair. "I should have thought to bring a raincoat." The pointless statement served to cut the tension in the air.

"It rained all the way here. The weatherman says we're in for a few days of it."

Jake turned onto the highway in the direction of the ranch, sloshing through standing water on the road. It had started raining during the night. He hadn't wanted to admit to Catherine that he'd picked her up from the airport because he'd been worried about her driving through the downpour.

That was a part of Jake's character that he couldn't change. He was used to handling things. Regardless of his feelings of betrayal and resentment, he would have been worried, knowing that Catherine was making her way to his ranch through poor weather on her own.

Jake told himself to keep his concentration on his driving. Unwillingly his thoughts shifted to the woman riding beside him. He hadn't figured on it being so hard to see Catherine again. He'd told himself that a lot of time had passed, that she wouldn't look like the young woman he'd fallen in love with.

And she didn't. That was a fact. If anything, she was more beautiful. He hadn't expected that, hadn't wanted to admit even to himself that he'd wondered about her since last night, but he had.

Jake stole a glance at Catherine, then quickly looked back at the highway, and his heart pumped just a little faster. The soft, musky scent of her perfume filled the inside of the truck.

Jake shook his head to dispel thoughts of how good Catherine looked to him, how good she smelled. She wasn't here to see him. She was here only because of Matthew.

Their son.

A tight coil of irritation swept through Jake every time he thought about the fact that he had a twelve-year-old son. He had to take a deep breath to quell the anger simmering inside him.

He'd never thought that Catherine had the power to hurt him, but he'd been wrong. Hadn't Maxine taught him a hard lesson? This time he wouldn't be so gullible. He would think with his head instead of his libido.

They traveled for a few more minutes when Jake spoke. His deep voice cut through the stark silence.

"The ranch is west of Crockett, which is a little farther down the road. It shouldn't take too long to get there."

Catherine nodded.

Obviously she was worried, if the way she was twisting her hands together was an indication. Jake told himself that he didn't care. Catherine wasn't his problem. She had no one to blame for this mess but herself. No, he wasn't about to feel sorry for her. Or attracted to her, he reminded himself.

"Did you tell Matthew that I was coming for him?" she asked. Her gaze landed on Jake and stayed there.

"He knows," Jake answered, not revealing that he and Matthew had discussed his mother's arrival in detail. Catherine was in for a surprise. Jake was torn between warning her and letting her face her son's determination on her own. He decided to say nothing. He didn't owe her a thing. She was the one who'd betrayed him. She was the one who hadn't told him he had a son.

"He's never done anything like this before." Catherine's voice quavered, and she gripped her upper arms with her hands. "I want you to know that he's a good boy."

Jake nodded slightly, but said nothing. He could think of a hundred things he wanted to say to Catherine, none of them particularly kind at the moment. He figured he was better off holding his tongue, at least until he came to grips with her deceit.

Catherine turned to look in Jake's direction, studying his profile as he stared straight ahead at the road. Her heart twisted painfully. The resemblance between father and son was striking, so much so that she couldn't have denied the truth if she'd wanted to. He had his father's height and build. No doubt her son would grow to look even more like Jake as the years passed.

Curiosity made her gaze drift to his strong hands gripping the steering wheel. He wasn't wearing a wedding ring. She had no idea of whether he was married or if he had other children. The fact that a ring was missing from his finger meant nothing. She supposed ranch work was hard and even sometimes dangerous. It was possible that he was married and didn't wear a ring. Catherine couldn't help but wonder.

"He's a good student in school," she said when he didn't reply.

Jake glanced at her briefly, seeming unwilling to make small talk. Finally he offered, "He seems to be a nice kid."

It was meant as a passing comment, rather than a compliment of her parenting skills. Catherine's carriage stiffened. Jake's hostility rankled her. It was *his* fault that he didn't know his son. *He* was the one who had left and never contacted her. "Look, I know this is an awkward situation."

That afforded her a hard look before he once again turned his attention to his driving and the rain pelting the windshield.

"That's putting it mildly."

Jake couldn't begin to tell Catherine how hard this was. Finding out he had a son had floored him. Learning that Catherine was Matt's mother was another huge shock. He hadn't thought he would ever see her again, or that she'd be so beautiful when he did. Or that he'd be so tempted to touch her.

He didn't like the way she affected him. He didn't like the familiar tug on his heart every time he looked at her. He opted to try to find out as much about her as he could, information that could prove to be useful to him in the future.

"Do you have other children?"

The personal question startled her. "No. I've never married. Matthew is my only child," she admitted.

Jake nodded casually, but her answer surprised him. Catherine was a lovely woman. He couldn't believe that some man hadn't snatched her up. Then he remembered that Matthew had mentioned his mother was getting married and that was the reason he'd run away from home. The boy had felt in the way. Jake wondered why.

"Matthew tells me that you're getting married, though," he commented, unable to stifle his curiosity.

"Matthew has been quite talkative," Catherine answered, neither confirming nor denying her relationship with Douglas. They'd talked about marriage, but she wasn't going to discuss her personal life with Jake.

"He said he didn't want to be in your way."

Catherine drew in a quick breath as her fingers touched her lips. "What?"

Jake glanced at her and saw raw pain register in her eyes. "He's upset and unhappy." It sounded like an accusation.

"He hasn't said a word to me. Until a month or so ago, I thought everything was fine." Catherine knew that Matthew didn't adore Douglas, but she'd thought they'd gotten along fine. She was surprised that her son had shared his innermost feelings with a stranger, be it his long-lost father or not.

"What happened then?" Jake questioned, wanting to know exactly where Matt was coming from. If Catherine had been a bad mother, it wasn't apparent.

Jake made the admission to himself grudgingly. No, he couldn't find fault with Matt's upbringing, except for the fact that he'd been able to slip away from his home unnoticed and travel miles away on his own.

Catherine shrugged her shoulders. "It's really nothing I can put my finger on. We didn't have a big argument or anything like that." She wished she could go back and relive the past, search for signs in her son that would have warned her of Matthew's rash decision to find his father.

"Matthew's always been a little quiet, so I didn't really notice a big change in his behavior."

"Something must have happened to upset him," Jake commented.

Catherine thought about it a moment. Suddenly a sinking feeling pulled at her chest and her heart ached. How could she not have realized? That was about the time she'd told Matthew that she and Douglas had discussed getting married.

When she'd brought the subject up, she hadn't thought the news would be a surprise to Matthew or that he would have this kind of reaction to it. She'd dated Douglas for almost a year. Matthew seemed to like him. When she'd asked how he felt about her getting married, Matthew had shrugged and said it was okay with him. To Catherine it had been a typical adolescent response.

"I talked with him about the possibility of my marrying Douglas," she finally said, hating to make the admission to Jake.

"Douglas?" Jake repeated, and his brow arched curiously.

Catherine flashed Jake a look, then glanced away, noticing that the rain had slackened a bit. "We've been friends for about a year, and I thought Matthew liked him. He's never given me any reason to suspect that he didn't," she assured Jake. Actually Matthew and Douglas *seemed* to get along. Catherine wondered if that had been planned on her son's part for her sake.

Though she did care for Douglas, she knew she wasn't wildly in love with him. But love had hurt her terribly once, and she had held back from giving her heart to another man. It didn't bother her that Douglas wasn't a particularly affectionate man. He had his interests, and Catherine had her own. She'd wanted Matthew to have a father figure to look up to.

How could she have been so wrong? she wondered now.

"Except by running away." The words sounded like an accusation. Jake didn't apologize.

Hurt etched Catherine's expression. "You're right," she admitted. Tears stung her eyes. "I should have seen that Matthew wasn't happy. I don't know how I missed it."

Jake hadn't meant to make her cry, and he didn't like feeling sorry for her. He had needed to distance himself from thinking about her feelings and he'd struck out automatically. "What do you plan to do now?" he asked, his voice gruff.

"I have to talk to Matthew before I decide anything," Catherine said, knowing there was no way she could marry Douglas. Her son was the most important thing in her life.

"What about you?" she asked, letting her gaze rest on Jake's ring-free hand as she sniffed back tears. He raised a dark-brown eyebrow. "Are you married?"

"No," Jake admitted, then added, "The timing was never right." He thought again of Maxine, how she'd reacted to his inability to father a child. She'd taught him a hard lesson. Bitterness swept through him. Over the years he'd had his share of women, but he hadn't been tempted to offer any of them more than a few months of his time and attention.

He glanced at Catie. Despite what she'd done, he did feel a sense of gratitude that he'd fathered Matthew before the accident. Still, he couldn't bring himself to admit to her that he had nothing to offer a woman, that he was unable to give a woman a child.

"Did you ever go back to school?" Catherine asked, pondering his answer. He was handsome, apparently successful and probably pleasant when he wasn't around her. The fact that he'd never married seemed strange to her.

Jake shook his head. "No. I had my hands full. First I had to be sure that my family had a roof over their heads and food to eat. Then there was the ranch to contend with. It was heavily mortgaged. I briefly thought of selling it and getting a job, but I couldn't. The ranch has been in the family for more years than I can count."

It sounded as if he'd sacrificed everything for his brothers and sister. A touch of sorrow filled Catherine's heart as she thought of such heavy responsibilities given to such a young man. Unfortunately, she told herself, she was one of the things that he'd sacrificed.

She'd thought she was over what had happened between them years ago. Matthew's recent actions, however, had dredged up old, painful memories. Memories that Catherine would have preferred not facing again.

"This is Crockett," Jake informed Catherine as they passed through a small town. "It's grown a lot in the last year." He indicated the new Wal-Mart, as well as a modern motel and a small shopping center. The rain let up slightly as Jake took a turn and headed up a paved road. "We'll be at the ranch in a few minutes."

Catherine nodded and tried to get a grip on her emotions. She didn't want Matthew to see her upset. Right now all she wanted was to put her arms around him and hug him tight.

"I'll warn you that we have a houseful. My brother

Ryder is married and lives at the ranch with his wife and twin daughters. His wife, Ashley, is expecting another baby in six months.''

Catherine noticed Jake's eyes soften when he spoke of his family and felt envious. Her father and mother had turned her away. She had hoped that over the years she would have heard from her younger sisters, but they hadn't answered any of her letters. Eventually she'd quit trying to contact them. She could only take a certain amount of rejection.

Jake watched Catherine's expression. She was quiet, listening to him without comment. He wondered what her life had been like. Had she had help with Matthew? He remembered her father was a preacher. Though he'd never met the man, Catie had said he was a rigid disciplinarian. Jake figured it must have been hard for her to tell her parents about her pregnancy. He was sorry about that. If he'd have known, he would have been there for her. He wondered if she knew that.

"I remember that you often talked about your brothers," she answered. "You have a younger sister, too, don't you?"

Jake nodded his head. "Yeah. Deke, my youngest brother, is away right now on the rodeo circuit. My little sister, Lynn, lives here also," he informed her.

"How little is she?" Catherine asked. Thinking back, Lynn had been a little girl when Catherine and Jake were in college.

A wry expression crossed Jake's features. "Not so little anymore. She's nineteen."

"That is quite a houseful," Catherine commented, wondering where all the years had gone. Jake seemed happy when talking about his siblings. "You're lucky to be so close to your family."

"I've always thought so." Jake didn't look at her as the car passed under the large wood-and-iron sign indicating they were on the Bar M ranch and nearing his house.

Catherine's teeth sank into her bottom lip. Now that they had arrived, she was even more anxious to see Matthew. Jake pulled up in front of a large ranch-style house and turned off the motor. He kept his hands on the wheel a moment longer, then turned in his seat.

"Family is the most important thing to me," he stated.

Something in the way he said the words made Catherine wince. Worry etched her brow.

Jake gave her an accusatory look. "Now I have a son that I knew nothing about. He's part of my family."

His words shook her to her very core. He was telling her that now that he knew about Matthew, he wasn't going to just forget that his son existed.

Oh, Matthew, Catherine thought. What kind of Pandora's box did you open?

Four

They'd arrived at the ranch at an opportune moment. The rain had almost stopped, Catherine noticed, but thick gray clouds in the overcast sky threatened more of a downpour. Jake got out of the vehicle and opened the back door to retrieve her bag. By the time he was around the opposite side of the car, she had her door open. Catherine got out and stepped away from him. As Jake turned to close the door, she ran a hand through her hair to smooth it, then surveyed her surroundings.

The McCall ranch was expansive, impressive to even one of novice knowledge of ranch life and all it entailed. There were several outbuildings—a large structure that housed ranch vehicles and equipment, and what she assumed were lodgings for employees.

As they drove in, she'd seen hundreds of cows in pastures and horses grazing in several fenced areas.

Catherine turned back toward Jake, who was watching her. She just as quickly looked away. "This is quite an operation," she commented, sounding impressed. "I can imagine why it takes your whole family to keep it going."

"There's always something to be done," he agreed, his tone matter-of-fact and not necessarily inviting further conversation.

Catherine looked around her, rubbing her hand against her thigh. Where was Matthew? she wondered, wanting to see her son.

"Let's go inside," Jake suggested, apparently reading her expression. "Watch your step," he said, indicating the rain-soft mud beside her. She'd already started to move, and Jake grabbed hold of her arm to save her from stepping right into a mud hole.

The action brought her back toward him, and Catherine found herself pressed against his body. His arm slipped around her to steady her. She lifted her face automatically and suddenly couldn't breathe. Jake's gaze raked her face, and in that moment Catherine wanted to press herself closer, to soak up his strength and warmth.

Jake didn't seem too pleased by their predicament. After a moment he moved away from her yet still held her arm. Catherine regained her footing, but her equilibrium had taken a beating. She felt a little dizzy and shook her head, trying to get her bearings.

"Thank you," she muttered. The brief contact between them had shaken her, and she didn't like it a bit. Without seeming ungracious, she pulled free of his grasp and stepped around the mud.

Jake walked beside her, and she noticed that he kept his distance. She wondered if he'd felt the same sense of longing that had attacked her in those few moments their bodies had touched.

The steps led to what looked like a newly constructed wooden porch. It was wide and wrapped around the expansive house. A large swing was suspended from hinges attached to the roof.

Jake glanced her way and said, "Ashley loves the outdoors. She was raised in the city, but I've never seen anyone take to country living the way she has. We had the porch constructed so she and Ryder could swing the twins. Sometimes it's the only thing that will calm them when they're fussy."

Catherine managed a smile. Jake had told her his twin nieces were adorable and warned her that they had the ability to steal hearts. She tried to imagine Jake holding an infant and comforting it. She couldn't bring a gentle image of him to mind. To her he was abrasive and distant.

But she could have sworn a moment ago that something akin to awareness had passed through his eyes when he'd caught her to him. He had an exceptional ability to hide his emotions. Something inside her wanted to break through his aloofness.

No, she reminded herself, that wouldn't do. She couldn't afford to let down her guard around Jake. She needed to remain focused. She needed to get her son and leave as soon as possible. She couldn't let old feelings for Jake blur her main objective.

Jake opened a screened door and motioned Catherine ahead of him without touching her. She walked inside and drew a deep breath as he followed her and removed his hat. He held it loosely in his hand.

From the foyer she could see that the house was

immaculate, well cared for and beautifully decorated with antiques.

"Your home is lovely," she said, and her tone implied that the compliment was genuine.

"Ashley usually takes care of it. However, now that she's pregnant again, we're looking to hire a housekeeper to come in daily."

"And I'm still not happy about that," a young woman said, smiling as she entered the foyer from a long hallway. She was very pretty, with long black hair and big brown eyes. She didn't look pregnant. Catherine would never have known if Jake hadn't mentioned it. "Hi. I'm Ashley, Ryder's wife. I see Jake brought you home safely."

Catherine smiled, for it was impossible not to. Jake's sister-in-law looked the picture of health and contentment.

"This is Catherine St. John," Jake said. "Matt's mother," he added as if it was an afterthought.

His tone was impersonal, not at all implying that there'd ever been an intimate relationship between them. Well, that was fine with her. She didn't want any reminders, either. She couldn't help wondering, though, how much Jake's family knew about their past.

"It's nice to meet you," Catherine offered. "I hope Matthew hasn't been a bother."

"Are you kidding?" Ashley asked. "He's been having the time of his life. Ryder took him when he rode out a while ago. They should be back any minute."

Concern crossed Catherine's expression. "Matthew doesn't know how to ride," she informed them, then looked at Jake. "I mean, not really. He's been horseback riding a few times with friends, but not very often."

"Take it easy," Jake said gruffly. "He's perfectly safe with Ryder. He'll take good care of him," he assured Catherine.

"Of course he will," Ashley chimed in. "I didn't mean to alarm you. Ryder gave him one of the gentler horses, and he didn't let Matthew hold the reins. I wish I'd had a camera," she continued. "Matthew was really excited."

That declaration brought a new concern to Catherine's mind, as if she didn't already have enough to worry about. She hadn't expected Matthew to be at Jake's long enough to sample any kind of ranch life. And the last thing she needed was for Matthew to actually like it here.

"Thank you for taking care of him," Catherine said, remembering her manners.

Ashley nodded. "It was our pleasure," she assured Catherine.

"Maybe you'd like a cup of coffee or something while you wait," Jake suggested, placing his hand against Catherine's back and urging her forward.

"Well—"

"Yes, of course," Ashley agreed. "Come on into the kitchen."

Catherine followed Ashley, feeling a bit bewildered. Once again Jake's touch had stirred long-buried emotions within her. She didn't want to feel any connection to him. Things weren't exactly going as she had planned.

"We've already had lunch," Ashley went on. "But I can quickly fix you something to eat if you'd like. Jake?" she inquired, looking his way.

"Nothing for me." Jake shook his head, but he flashed Ashley a brief smile.

Catherine was momentarily stunned. His smile had transformed Jake's detached expression, and she couldn't believe how much so. His gorgeous brown eyes sparkled at Ashley with love and admiration. Before Catherine could adjust to the sudden change that came over Jake, the stoic look that had accompanied him from San Luis had returned.

"Catherine?"

"Um, no, thank you. Maybe just some coffee."

Ashley nodded and poured them each a cup. She offered one to Catherine, then indicated for her to take a seat at the kitchen table. Catherine slid onto a seat, then wrapped her hands around the warm mug just to give them something to do.

Jake remained standing, and Catherine couldn't keep from watching him as Ashley passed him a cup. It was obvious that she held a warm place in his heart.

Ashley slid into a chair and breathed deeply. "How were the roads?" she asked, looking at Jake.

"Slick." Jake set his cup on the counter.

Catherine nodded. "We saw several accidents on the way here," she commented. "I hope it won't be too long before we can start back."

Jake flashed her a questionable look. "I doubt if that will be possible."

Catherine's gaze darted to his. "What?"

"I don't think we'll be driving back this evening."

Was he kidding? she wondered. "But you said you'd take us back right away."

Jake shook his head. "What I said was, if you wanted to return right away, I'd take you back. I didn't plan on the rain preventing us from driving back."

"The rain?" she repeated. "Why would it?" Catherine asked, confused.

"The Styron bridge for one thing," Jake stated, glancing at Ashley, then back at Catherine. "Didn't you notice that the river was running high on both sides as we crossed over it on the way?"

Catherine looked surprised. She'd been so worried about Matthew that she hadn't paid much attention. "Actually, no, I didn't."

"We've had a lot of rain over the past few days. It could be dangerous crossing back over the bridge. We made it here okay, but that doesn't mean that by the time we drive back it'll be safe."

Before anyone spoke again, they heard a deafening crack of thunder. The screened door banged open, then a door slammed. Anticipation kept Catherine's next breath captive. Moments later Matthew walked into the kitchen ahead of Jake's brother. They were both damp from the rain.

"Hi, Mom," Matthew said, then tentatively stepped toward his mother. Catherine was already out of her seat and met her son in the middle of the kitchen. She threw her arms around his neck and hugged him to her.

Then she cried.

Catherine couldn't help it. Relief swept through her. Matthew hugged her briefly, then, looking embarrassed, stepped back away from her. Catherine ran her hand over his head and across his cheek, letting her palm rest there a moment.

"I was so worried about you." She wanted to hold him to her, but was wise enough to realize that Matthew didn't want to be treated like a child. Sheer willpower kept her from hugging him to her again.

"I'm okay," Matthew insisted. "Ryder took me riding." He said it with a big grin as he glanced at Jake's brother, whom it was apparent he already idolized.

Jake introduced them, and Ryder nodded. He didn't look like Jake at all. He was only a tad taller, but his hair was blond and he had gorgeous blue eyes. His smile, accompanied by his blond mustache, immediately charmed her.

"Matt's a natural," he informed Catherine, as he stood behind Ashley with his hands on her shoulders.

Catherine nodded and forced a smile. Silence filled the room.

Ashley started to get up, and Ryder helped her to her feet. "I think I hear the girls." She looked at Ryder, then back to Catherine. "Excuse us, please." Taking his cue, Ryder followed his wife out of the room.

A bolt of lightning flashed outside the kitchen window, followed closely by the roar of thunder. It briefly vibrated the walls around them. Catherine turned worried eyes toward her son. "Matthew, get your things. We need to head back right away."

Matthew didn't move. He took a step away from her, closer to Jake. "I don't want to go back," he declared.

Stunned, Catherine's hand went to her chest as the agony of his words hit her. "Matthew—"

"You can't make me!" He looked at the floor instead of at his mother, reminding her of the troubled teens she often dealt with at school.

Catherine reached toward her son. "Matthew, of course you're going home with me." What was he talking about? For heaven's sake, he was only twelve years old. He wasn't old enough to know what was best for him.

"I like it here," Matthew said.

"That's ridiculous," Catherine blurted out, then wished she'd held back the words. She didn't want to put Matthew on the defensive. This wasn't the time or place to discipline him for his behavior. "You've only been here twenty-four hours. You don't know anything about living on a ranch."

Matthew stuck out his chin. "I can learn."

Catherine tried desperately to remain calm. She glanced at Jake, who stood nearby, taking in their conversation. Something in his expression disturbed her. She turned her attention to her son. "Look, I know we have some things to talk about, but we can work this out at home."

"Please, Mom, let me stay," Matthew said, and his gaze pleaded with her.

Catherine closed her eyes for a moment and wished for this nightmare to end. She opened her eyes and pinned her gaze on her son. "I'm not going to argue with you about this. Go and get your things." Even as she said the words, she knew she'd made a mistake.

Matthew's carriage stiffened. "If you take me back, I'll just run away again."

"Matt, that's enough," Jake broke in as he took in Catherine's shocked expression. Tears gathered at the corners of her eyes. "Why don't you go watch television or something and let your mother and I talk?" he suggested.

Without having to be convinced, Matthew left before Catherine could prevent him. She was amazed that Jake had such control over her son after only one night in his home. Suddenly she was very worried.

"I don't know what's come over him," Catherine whispered. "He's never been defiant before."

"There's a lot going on in his life right now," Jake reasoned. "He's confused. Give him some time."

Catherine's gaze met Jake's. "You're not suggesting that I leave him here?" She searched his face. "You *knew* he was going to give me a hard time,'' she accused. Jake didn't deny it. ''You could have warned me.''

''Like you warned me that I had a son? Be honest, Catherine. You didn't really think you could just show up here, whisk Matt away and pretend that none of this had happened, did you?'' Jake leaned against the edge of the sink, looking at her with an accusing stare.

Catherine folded her arms about her and looked away. Jake *knew* that's exactly what she'd planned. ''I expected Matthew to talk to me.'' Her gaze went back to Jake. ''What have you said to him?'' she questioned.

''Only that we'd discuss the situation and work something reasonable out,'' Jake told her.

''There's nothing to work out,'' she insisted, resolving not to cry. ''I'm taking my son home.'' Her voice rose a notch.

''Let's finish this conversation in the office,'' Jake suggested. Jake wanted to be sure Matthew wasn't within hearing distance of their discussion. He turned and walked out, leaving Catherine behind. She had no choice but to follow.

They went down the hallway, then into a large room. The office was filled with modern-day devices. One wall was completely taken up with a computer, table, a printer and a fax machine. In the middle of the room was a massive walnut desk. Jake motioned for Catherine to sit down. She chose a seat on the large brown sofa.

Jake leaned against the edge of the desk, and Catherine couldn't help thinking he did so to put her at a disadvantage. She had to look up at him.

''I think we need to get a few things out in the

open.'' Jake's tone left no doubt as to what he was talking about.

Catherine had to agree. She nodded and waited. Jake owed her an explanation. Not that anything he said would excuse the letter his attorney had sent her.

For a few moments silence reigned between them. Finally Catherine said, ''Well?'' If he was going to apologize, he wasn't making any headway in that direction.

Jake's face wrinkled a bit. ''Well what?'' he countered. ''I think you're the one who has something to say.''

''Me?'' Catherine almost laughed. ''I'm waiting for *your* explanation,'' she insisted. ''You're the one who never called me back.''

Jake stared at her. ''I don't know what you're talking about.''

Catherine looked aghast. ''I called you, Jake. Several times. I left messages, but you never returned my calls. Why not?'' she asked. Despite her resolve to remain aloof, her emotions betrayed her. She remembered how alone and desperate she'd felt when she hadn't heard from him.

''I didn't get any messages,'' Jake insisted, standing and approaching her.

He sounded as if he didn't believe her. Catherine stood as he came nearer and stopped in front of her. ''I can't help that. I called,'' she insisted. Regardless of whether he'd received her messages, there was the letter she'd written. He'd dismissed her as if she never really mattered to him.

Jake didn't give an inch. ''A couple of phone calls hardly excuses the fact that you kept Matt's birth a secret all these years.''

Catherine's mouth gaped open. Finally she said, "You've got a nerve, Jake McCall." Fuming, she balled her hands beside her, trying very hard to keep her temper intact.

Jake's expression hardened. "Me?"

"Yes, you!" The anger and disappointment of twelve long years filled her. "I sent you a letter."

"I never received a letter from you."

Dismissing his answer, Catherine said, "I asked you to contact me. I didn't want to tell you about my being pregnant in a letter, for heaven's sake! If you'd bothered to call me, you would have known about Matthew, wouldn't you?" she accused. She wanted, needed to know why he hadn't contacted her.

Jake's jaw tightened. "And the fact that I didn't call you excuses your actions," he answered. He leaned forward, causing Catherine to retreat a step. It put her against the sofa.

"I don't need an excuse for my actions," she stated tightly. His breath fanned her face and she could smell his aftershave. Suddenly she very much needed some space between them. Scooting around him, she walked over to the desk and touched it briefly. Then she faced him.

"I sent you a letter, Jake," she said again, and her voice became low and filled with years of sadness. She shivered and closed her arms around herself. "You wrote back that I was never to contact you again."

Jake raked a hand through his hair, frustration driving the movement. "That's crazy. I never sent you a letter like that." When he looked at her, his expression changed. "I would never had done that. Hell, Catie, you knew me better than anyone."

Catherine only looked at him with disappointment.

"I thought I did." Suddenly she wanted to cry. But she didn't.

Jake put his hands in his back pockets to keep them from reaching toward her. "Do you still have this letter?" he asked, patience lacking in his tone.

Defiantly Catherine's gaze locked with his. "You don't believe me." Her laugh was forced. "Well, that's just dandy. You think you'd remember having your lawyer send me a letter."

"My lawyer?" Jake stopped speaking to think a moment. Back then, the only lawyer he knew was his parents' lawyer. "You got a letter from Frank Davis?"

"As if you didn't know," she replied.

"Catherine, I don't know anything about a letter. I swear it. Frank Davis was my parents' lawyer. Shortly after I came home, he had all the mail sent to his office. He handled all the correspondence and bills while I learned everything I needed to know to keep the ranch afloat."

The ranch hadn't been in the best of conditions when Jake had taken over. He had always admired his father, but he never really knew how much the man struggled until he died. There'd been a drought that year, and cattle prices had dropped drastically. His father had worked hard for years, only to end up in debt and struggling to hang on to their land.

Jake's admiration of his father had taken a nosedive when he'd learned that he'd been the result of his father's adulterous affair. Jake stiffened as he thought about when he'd first learned the truth. Then he pushed the bad feelings to the back of his mind. He refused to let it haunt him today.

His gaze fell on Catherine, who had walked across the room to stare out at the rain beating against the window. She jumped when lightning flashed across the sky. He called to her and she turned toward him. "If Frank wrote you, I didn't know about it," he said again. Jake looked closer and saw tears fall down her cheeks.

"The letter said you didn't know me."

Jake expression changed to one of shock and disbelief. "Why would Frank do something like that?" Jake wondered aloud. Jake wasn't used to having his word questioned. "Does that even sound like something I'd do?" he asked, walking toward her.

Catherine didn't think before she answered, "Yes."

Her words stopped Jake dead in his tracks. "You believe I would deny knowing you?" he asked, anger in his voice.

"We'd argued right before you left to go home, so I believed you didn't want anything to do with me." And if he hadn't wanted her, he wouldn't have wanted their baby. She hadn't wanted Jake to come back to her out of a sense of responsibility. She'd wanted his love. She glared at him, then said, "Look, this is getting us nowhere. I don't see why we have to hash out the past. I came here to get my son and I intend to leave with him."

"We need to get to the bottom of this. Frank Davis died, but we can probably get access to his files." Before Catherine could answer, there was a knock at the door. It cracked open, and Ashley's head appeared.

"I'm sorry for interrupting." She stepped farther into the room. "Matthew's missing. Ryder's gone outside to look for him."

Jake had only a moment to register Catherine's distressed look before he bolted for the door. "Damn," he swore, then looked at Ashley. "Did you call the men?'' he asked, referring to the hands who stayed on the ranch.

"I wanted you to know first."

Jake brushed past her and headed for the back door. "I'll take care of it," he said over his shoulder.

"Jake, wait," Catherine called. "I'm going with you." She caught up with him as he was putting his arms though the sleeves of his raincoat.

"No, you're not," Jake stated firmly. "You don't know the ranch well enough to go off on your own, and I don't have time to keep an eye on you."

Insulted, Catherine bristled. "I'm an adult. You don't have to watch out for me. But I'm going out to find Matthew," she insisted.

"Catherine, just wait here."

"He's right," Ashley said softly, putting her hand on the other woman's shoulder. "Matthew might come back. One of you should be here."

Catherine couldn't argue with Ashley's reasoning. "All right," she said, relenting.

Jake headed out the back door. "I'll let you know as soon as we find him."

Pushing against the wind, Ashley closed the door. "Don't worry," she said. "Matthew couldn't have gone far. They'll find him." She led Catherine back to the kitchen and ushered her to a chair.

Ashley poured them both coffee. Catherine accepted a cup, then Ashley sank onto a chair across from her. "Try not to worry. I'm sure they'll find him."

Catherine shook her head back and forth. "I don't know what's come over Matthew. He's never acted like this before."

"Sometimes children, like adults, have trouble expressing their feelings. Matthew's just mixed up right now.''

For such a young woman, Catherine thought, Ashley was very wise. ''You'd make a great counselor,'' she told her.

''Is that what you do?'' Ashley asked.

Catherine nodded. ''I'm a counselor at a high school.'' She brought her hand up and wiped tears from her eyes. ''You'd think I'd do a better job of understanding my own child.''

Ashley's expression filled with sympathy. ''I'm sure you're a wonderful mother. Matthew's a very polite young man. You should be proud of the job you've done.''

Catherine managed a small smile. She wanted to think that she was a good mother, but she'd been having a lot of doubts over the past twenty-four hours.

Seeing how Matthew responded to Jake hadn't helped. Her son had quickly implanted himself in this home, with his father. Catherine wasn't sure what was going to happen next, but she didn't like the feeling of foreboding that hung over her.

The back door opened and Catherine turned to see Matthew, Jake and Ryder enter. She was on her feet and standing, by the time they walked into the kitchen. Matthew was soaking wet, dripping on the vinyl floor.

''Matthew, what on earth has gotten into you?'' she demanded. Realizing she probably sounded hysterical, she took a deep breath and stepped back, her gaze running over him.

Jake spoke instead of Matthew. ''The good news is we found Matt. He was in the barn.'' Taking off his coat and shaking the water from it, he added, "The bad news is that we just heard over the radio that the Styron bridge is impassable." Looking directly at Catherine, he told her, "You're stuck here."

Five

Stuck, Catherine learned, meant that she and Matthew weren't getting back to Lubbock anytime in the immediate future. She stood in the bedroom she'd been shown to and took stock of her situation. Jake told her that once it quit raining, it could be a few days before the water receded enough for them to cross the bridge.

Catherine was glad she'd had the foresight to bring a change of clothing with her and something to sleep in.

She supposed she would be able to wear the same two sets of clothing for a few days, until they were ready to leave. She'd rinse out her underwear and hang them in the bathroom to dry.

Jake's sister, Lynn, had brought Catherine to Ryder's old bedroom so she could have an adjoining bath. Matthew had been moved to Deke's room, since he wasn't home.

Lynn looked a lot like her brother Ryder. Her blond hair was cropped short, and she had the same beautiful blue eyes. She was pretty and petite and very outgoing and friendly.

Nothing at all like Jake, who gave Catherine cold stares and frustrated looks most of the time. He thought she was at fault for the current crisis in his life, and from what she could gather, Jake wasn't used to being the center of attention. Neither was he used to not having everything under control.

Well, Jake was going to learn he couldn't control her. As soon as the weather allowed, she and Matthew were leaving—if she had to steal a car to drive to the airport!

Catherine glanced at her watch and realized she should be getting ready for dinner. Lynn had refused her offer of help, insisting that she and Ashley were used to working together in the kitchen, but Catherine was welcome to come in and talk with them.

She headed for the bathroom to wash up, then she would accept Lynn's offer. Though part of her wanted to, she couldn't just hide here in the bedroom until the weather let up and she could go home.

Catherine reached for the handle of the bathroom door and swung it open, then caught her breath at the sight of Jake standing at the sink, naked to his waist. His jeans rested low on his hips, exposing his navel. Lather partially covered his face, and he held a razor in his hand.

"Oh!" she exclaimed, her gaze taking in his hard-muscled shoulders and chest. For a man in his thirties, he was in excellent condition. Catherine glanced at the open door behind him, then back at Jake. Apparently the bathroom serviced both bedrooms. "I didn't know…um…"

Jake raised an eyebrow. "That we were sharing a bath?" he furnished, his voice a bit husky. His dark gaze slipped over her as he set down the razor and grabbed a towel off the rack on the wall. He looked at her as he cleaned off what remained of the lather from his face.

"It's just as much my fault. I'm not used to anyone being in that room, and I don't usually check the door," he admitted gruffly.

"I'll just wait," Catherine said, her breathing constricted. She started to close the door.

"No, that's all right," Jake said, stalling her movements. "I'm about finished." He dried his hands on the towel and tossed it on the counter. "There are fresh linens in here," he said, opening a small closet door and removing a clean towel and washcloth. His shirt was hanging on the doorknob to his room, and he picked it up and shrugged into it.

Catherine watched his muscles ripple as he moved, her heartbeat speeding. Jake was nothing at all like Douglas: his body was hard and tanned; his chest lightly covered with soft brown hair that about disappeared across his flat belly.

What would it feel like to touch him there? she wondered, remembering the days when she could freely do so. As he buttoned his shirt, Catherine looked away, her gaze resting on the mirror. His reflection shared the details as he slipped each button through its matching hole. His gaze connected with hers as she watched him, and Catherine could have died at that moment. She blushed furiously.

"I think we need to finish our conversation," he said, leaning against the small counter.

"Um, yes, of course," Catherine said, agreeing. There was so much more she wanted to say to him. But the tight, intimate confines of the bathroom was definitely not the place.

He reached around her for a small bottle, bringing his body in close contact with hers. He smelled of soap and shaving cream, amazingly male, and to Catherine it was an awesome mix. She watched him dump a small amount of cologne in his hands, then pat his face.

"Maybe after dinner?" she suggested. "I was just going to go down and see if I could help."

Jake nodded, watching her a moment longer before turning away. "Fine." He stood and walked out of the bathroom, then closed the connecting door.

Behind it, he heard Catherine moving about. He ignored the sound of running water, but a vision of her filled his mind. He wished he could ignore how his body responded when he was around her. He'd thought that all he would have to do was keep her at arm's length.

Their brief contact upon their arrival had told Jake to be leery of Catherine. In the flash of a few moments her body had pressed close to his and he'd wanted to pull her tighter against him. He'd had to steel himself not to.

Now he was sharing a bathroom with her. Close quarters for someone who wanted to keep his distance. He reminded himself that she wasn't the vulnerable, innocent young woman he'd made love to years ago. But somehow, his body wasn't accepting his explanation.

She was able to bring out many emotions that he'd

managed to keep to himself for most of his life. Since she'd arrived, he'd wanted to both comfort her, kiss her and strangle her within a single conversation.

They still needed to come to some kind of agreement where his son was concerned. Whether the lady knew it or not, Jake had already decided exactly what was best for all of them. At the very least, Matthew was going to spend his summer here at the ranch.

Catherine didn't have to like it. She just had to agree to it. The weather had given him an advantage. Keeping Catherine and Matthew here for a day or so was exactly what he needed. A little time and he'd be able to convince her that it was in Matt's best interest to let him stay.

Jake wasn't beyond demanding that his son live with him permanently. First, he had to get Matt settled here on the ranch. Then he'd have more leverage.

Having Catherine here for a few days could prove a test to his patience, though, and his libido. He'd fallen for her so easily when he'd first met her. He wasn't going to make the same mistake again.

So what if he still felt an attraction toward her. It had been quite a while since he'd been with a woman. That his body was suddenly responding sexually to an attractive woman wasn't unusual. It could have been any woman and he'd have had the same reaction, he told himself.

Catherine looked as if she spent time keeping herself in shape, no doubt for this man she was planning to marry. Jake just had to keep reminding himself that he could be around Catherine, even be attracted to her, and it wouldn't have to lead anywhere.

By keeping Matthew a secret she'd hurt Jake, and he couldn't forget or forgive that. Just as he couldn't forget his father's indiscretion. Every time he looked at his siblings, he knew how hurt they'd be if they found out. Jake couldn't share what he knew with them.

Catherine went in search of Matthew and found him in the den watching a sports event on television. She talked with him about what he'd done and how dangerous it was for him to travel on his own. There were so many things that could have happened to him. Matthew listened, and it was apparent that he was sorry for his actions and that he'd worried her so much.

He asked her again to let him stay at the ranch. Catherine tried to reason with him, to make him understand that his life was in Lubbock, not here on this ranch. Matthew was having none of it. By the time she left him alone, he'd become sullen and withdrawn. She was right back where she'd started.

Catherine walked into the kitchen after her talk with Matthew, and a smile crossed her features. Earlier, she hadn't noticed the playpen cluttered with toys. At the moment, two little dark-headed babies shared what room was left. Ashley and Lynn were moving about the room.

Both little faces looked in her direction as she walked over to the playpen, their angelic smiles welcoming the stranger entering their world.

"Oh my, they're adorable," Catherine exclaimed, her gaze running over them. Each one was standing and holding on to the side of the pen.

Ashley smiled. "That they are," she agreed. "They're also quite a handful. They look perfectly innocent," she went on, "but don't believe it."

Lynn grinned and said, "They're angels with minds of their own."

"Just like every true McCall," Ashley commented.

"Can't disagree with that," Lynn answered.

Catherine ran her hand over each baby's head and was rewarded with smiles and gurgles from them. "What are their names?" she asked.

Ashley pointed at one of them. "That's Michelle with her hand in Melissa's hair."

Catherine helped free Melissa's hair from the baby's grasp. "Can I hold one of them?" she asked. It had been a long time since she'd held a baby. Ashley grinned and nodded, and Catherine picked up Melissa. She hugged the baby to her, and Melissa rested her head on Catherine's shoulder.

Jake picked that moment to walk into the room. He took stock of everyone, his gaze finally coming to rest on Catherine. His heart thudded. He wasn't prepared for the sight of her holding one of the babies.

She was cradling Melissa in her arms, and he had a sudden image of her holding his son as a baby. Jake walked over and scooped Michelle up in his arms. Giving her a quick kiss, he patted her back. Michelle giggled and drew a smile from him.

Catherine watched the byplay between Jake and the baby and was sorry about how much of Matthew's life Jake had missed. Of course, she reminded herself, it was his own fault. Still, she felt a sadness for him. Those years were gone now, never to be regained.

"Dinner will be ready shortly," Ashley announced. She looked at Jake and Catherine. "Would you mind putting them in their cribs for me? If we're lucky, they'll settle down right about the time we eat."

Jake nodded. Dinners, which used to be around six,

had been moved to seven and sometimes later to accommodate the babies' schedules. Most of the time they went to sleep about the time the adults ate and remained quiet for the night. The trade-off was that they were early risers. Ashley and Ryder usually went to bed early also, anticipating the morning when they'd be busy with the babies.

Jake motioned Catherine to follow him, and led her to a bedroom filled with baby items. There were two of everything, as if items could only be purchased that way.

"How many bedrooms does this house have?" she asked, surprised that this was another one she hadn't seen.

"Not enough if Ryder doesn't stop reproducing," Jake said, cracking a quick smile. It was gone after only a moment. "When the new baby arrives, it'll stay in Ryder and Ashley's bedroom for a while. We may have to put an addition on."

They put the babies in their cribs. Jake kissed each one, then walked toward the door. Michelle fretted, wanting to be picked up, but Melissa lay quietly in the middle of the crib looking at them with big, expressive eyes.

"Give your mom a break and go to sleep," Jake gently ordered the two little ones. He walked out of the room, then waited for Catherine.

By the time they arrived back in the kitchen, Ryder was helping Ashley and Lynn set the dining room table. Even Matthew was lending a hand. He barely looked at his mother, and Catherine felt hurt surge through her.

Dinner conversation went smoothly enough, considering the fact that Catherine avoided eye contact with

Jake. Though he answered questions when spoken to, Matthew was quiet and noncommunicative. After they finished eating, everyone carried their dishes into the kitchen. Lynn shooed everyone out, insisting that it didn't take all of them to stack the dishwasher. Ryder and Matthew went to the den to watch television. Ashley confessed she'd been looking forward to a long, hot bath.

That left Jake and Catherine alone to finish their conversation from earlier in the day. Once again Catherine followed him to the ranch office. He closed the door for privacy.

Jake sat on the sofa, then waited for Catherine to take a seat. She joined him, surprising him by sitting on the other end instead of one of the chairs. She folded her hands together tightly, looking as tense as a person being robbed at gunpoint.

"Sit back," Jake said, leaning forward and closer to her. "I'm not going to eat you."

She didn't seem amused by his words. He was trying to put her at ease. He figured they'd get along better if she didn't think she was under attack.

"I don't want to rehash what we went through this afternoon," Catherine stated, starting the conversation. "Obviously we both have different views of what happened between us years ago."

Her words conjured up images in Jake's mind of making love to her. It wasn't hard for Jake to recall how good they'd been together. His body reacted in kind, and he shifted a little in his seat. He couldn't afford to let his mind wander so easily.

"Obviously," he agreed. He still had trouble with her story.

"And it has little bearing on the current problem we're facing with Matthew," Catherine reasoned.

"I agree." Jake wasn't ready to let the past go. He still blamed Catie for keeping his son from him. But the most important thing for them to talk about now was what was best for Matthew.

Catherine sighed heavily, and her gaze met Jake's. "Please don't fight me on this, Jake," she pleaded. "I think the best thing for Matthew is for us to go home and pick up where we left off."

"I don't think so," Jake stated, then rested his arm along the back of the sofa. "That's what's best for you. You're not even thinking about what's best for Matthew or me."

Catherine licked her lips, and Jake's gaze followed the movement of her tongue. He remembered kissing her, touching her skin, and had a sudden urge to see if she still tasted the way he remembered.

"I'm not saying that you can't see him," she told him. "But I don't want Matthew to get the idea that he can call this ranch his home."

"This *is* his home. Matthew's my son. That makes him part of this family. Someday he'll own his share of the ranch." He sat forward, leaning closer to her. "What's more important, I have a son that I've never had the opportunity to know. We need time together to bond, time to enjoy each other. Are you going to deny us that?"

"Of course not," Catherine assured him.

"Then, what better place to do it than here," Jake said, his gaze pinning hers.

Silence filled the room for a moment. Then Jake told her what he really wanted. "I want Matthew to spend the summer with me."

"The summer?" Catherine looked stunned.

"School's out," Jake reminded her. "There's no reason why he can't stay here for the summer. That would solve this problem of him threatening to run away."

"No," Catherine replied, after absorbing Jake's suggestion. "Absolutely not. I'm not leaving Matthew here for the entire summer. That's out of the question."

Jake gritted his teeth, clamping down on the spark of anger that flared within him. He tried to reason with her. "Think about it, Catie," he told her, realizing that he'd slipped back to using her nickname. "He's already fighting you about going back. What could it hurt?"

Losing control, Catherine's eyes welled with tears. "Oh, Jake." Her breath caught and she bit her lip.

Automatically Jake reached over and touched her hand, cupping his around it. His thumb stroked back and forth. "What?" he asked.

His gaze searched her face, and he forgot they were talking about their son. For a moment, just seconds, he had the sudden urge to pull her into his arms. Jake shook his head, clearing the uninvited thought away.

Catherine ran a hand through her hair, getting it out of her way. "I'm afraid," she confessed. "What if he loves it here?" she asked. "What if he never wants to come home?" There was so much at the ranch to entertain him, so much to entice a young boy.

"Why don't we worry about that when the time comes."

Catherine snatched her hand back. "That's easy for you to say!" She stared back at him defiantly. "You've got nothing to lose!"

Jake's shoulders squared. "I've already lost twelve

years," he retorted, beginning to lose his temper. "I'm not losing another day," he told her, his voice rising. He got to his feet. "Now, you can agree to this and save us all a lot of trouble, or I'll have my lawyer take you to court," he challenged.

Catherine was on her feet in barely a second. "Don't threaten me, Jake!"

"Don't make me," he countered, leaning closer to her. His hand grasped the back of her neck, pulling her toward him. "I won't lose, I can promise you."

"Damn you," she stated hotly, glaring back at him.

Jake stared into her eyes. The fire in them fueled his desire to taste her. Jake was reminded of a couple of heated arguments they'd had when they were together—after they'd made up, they'd made love.

"Damn you," he grated, then covered her mouth with his.

It was a fool thing to do, he told himself, even as he tugged her closer to prevent her from breaking away. She fought him for a moment, her body stiff and resistant, her hands against his chest. Jake felt the heat of her palms as she pushed against him.

His tongue seared hers and she groaned low in her throat. It was all the encouragement he needed to drag her body against his and close his arms around her.

She tasted sweet, like honey. He remembered the first time he'd made love to her. She'd been a virgin and unsure of what to expect. But she'd also been eager to learn and just as eager to please him.

And one of the times they'd made love, she'd conceived his son.

The thought flitted through Jake's mind, clearing the way for rational thinking. He lifted his head and stared at Catherine's face. Her lids slowly slid open, and her eyes were glazed. She licked at her lips, and the action made his knees want to buckle.

With a slight movement, Jake pushed her away from him. ''This doesn't change anything,'' he grated, angry at himself for touching her. Angry, also, because he wanted to kiss her again.

Catherine glared back at him, looking confused, as if she'd been in a coma and was just waking up.

''Think about what I said,'' he warned her, then he stalked out of the room.

Catherine stared after him, still shell-shocked. He'd taken her by surprise when he'd kissed her. And like a complete fool, she kissed him back.

Idiot! she berated herself.

How could she have let him touch her? How could she have succumbed so easily to his embrace? Did he think he could seduce her, then talk her into his plan?

No, she thought, he didn't seem any too happy with the kiss they'd shared than she was. It was the heat of the moment, she decided. First they were yelling at each other, then he was kissing her. It just happened. That didn't mean that it would happen again.

She wouldn't let it, she decided. So he kissed her. So the memory of how good they'd been together haunted her. So what?

By the time Catherine got her bearings, Jake was long gone. She left the office and headed for her room to think. She wasn't going to give that kiss another moment of thought.

Jake had meant what he said. Now she was trapped in this house with him, with his ultimatum. Not only did she have Matthew begging her to let him stay, now his father was telling her she had no choice.

Catherine went in search of Matthew. Despite his

distant attitude, she hugged him good-night and told him she'd talk to him tomorrow. Right now she couldn't even think of what to say. She had to deal with Jake first. It would do no good to bring her son into it.

She made her way to her room and closed the door, exhausted and ready for bed. She wasn't sure where Jake was, so she leaned her head against the door to the bathroom to see if he was there. No sound came from behind the door. She opened it and was relieved to find it empty.

Catherine rushed in. She locked both doors, then washed her face and patted it dry. Then she unlocked Jake's door and returned to her room.

She crawled into bed with a heavy heart. Whether she wanted to admit it or not, Jake held all the cards. She had no idea what a judge would say if she tried to fight him and they ended up in court. Most times, judges still favored mothers. But the fact that Jake hadn't known about his son, and that Matthew wanted to live here, would probably work against her.

Not to mention that Jake had the monetary resources to tie her up in court. She'd end up losing everything trying to hold on to her son. To Catherine, nothing was more important than Matthew.

Catherine sighed and rubbed her temples with her fingers. The last day and a half had taken its toll on her. She no longer heard the rain and prayed that it had stopped. Maybe she could hold Jake off, pretend to consider his suggestion, then take Matthew and leave when he wasn't looking.

That was her best plan, she thought. Pathetically, it was her only plan. Catherine sank deeper into the mattress and stretched, trying to ease the tenseness in her body. She closed her eyes and took a breath in an effort to relax. It was an hour before she was able to fall asleep.

The next morning Catherine awoke early, something unexplainable tugging at her consciousness. Quiet surrounded her and she lay still, trying to figure out what was different.

It wasn't raining, she realized. She jumped from the bed and ran to the window. Luck was on her side. The sun was just beginning to shine, and the sky was clear and blue.

Thank God, she thought, for lousy weather predictions. She knew it didn't mean that she could leave with Matthew today, of course, but she could within a day or so.

She listened at the bathroom door again to be sure Jake wasn't there, then opened the door. After locking the door to his bedroom, Catherine stripped off her nightgown and turned on the water for a shower.

She rushed through her bath, dried her hair, applied light makeup, then unlocked Jake's door before returning to her room to dress. After pulling on a pair of jeans, she slipped on a T-shirt and sneakers, then went down the hallway toward the kitchen.

The house was deserted, except for Ashley and the babies. Catherine found them in the den, both babies on the floor. One was rolling over and the other was inching toward the door. Catherine caught her as she was about to escape. She scooped the baby up and into her arms, then greeted Ashley.

"Good morning," she said, laughing at the cherub in her arms.

Ashley looked relieved. "Thanks for detaining Michelle," she answered, smiling.

"You're welcome. How do you tell them apart?"

Chuckling, Ashley explained, "Mainly by their personalities. Michelle's more demanding than her sister. Also, we think Michelle is right-handed and Melissa's left-handed."

"Really?"

"It isn't unusual for twins to exhibit mirror-image features. Can I get you some breakfast?"

Catherine declined. "I'll just have coffee or some juice."

"There's coffee ready to pour," Ashley informed her. She got up and reached for Michelle, relieving Catherine of her rambunctious daughter.

"Thanks. Where is everyone?" Catherine asked, wanting to know where Matthew was.

"Ranch life starts early. Everyone's eaten and gone out. Lynn's working with the foreman. They're in charge of the horses—or rather, to Lynn's dismay, Russ Logan, the foreman is. Jake and Ryder have gone out, too, doing whatever needs their attention." She smiled. "And in answer to your next question, Matthew is down at the corral, watching Lynn and Russ."

"Oh. Well, I guess I'll get that coffee. Can I pour you some?"

Ashley shook her head. "No, thanks, but I'll join you for conversation if it's okay."

Catherine nodded. "Sure. Can I bring one of the babies?"

"I've got Michelle, if you can get Melissa."

They went into the kitchen and deposited the babies in the playpen. Both girls attacked their toys as if it was the first time they'd seen them.

Catherine followed Ashley's directions to locate a cup, then poured herself some hot coffee. She joined Ashley at the table.

"When do you think the bridge will be passable?" Catherine asked the younger woman.

Ashley shrugged. "One or two days if the weather is nice and the sun keeps shining. I guess you're anxious to go home?"

"Yes," Catherine acknowledged.

"I don't mean to be nosy, but have you and Jake agreed on what to do about Matthew?" Ashley asked. "Jake told me what he proposed," she confessed.

"He did?" Catherine was sure Jake didn't tell Ashley he'd actually demanded that she leave Matthew for the summer.

Ashley put her cup down. "He mentioned it before going out this morning, but not in front of Matthew," she said. "He seemed so quiet this morning. I wondered if the two of you had a fight."

Catherine frowned. "We did, sort of."

"Jake's taking all this rather badly," Ashley furnished. "He's usually very agreeable and easygoing."

"I have a hard time believing that," Catherine admitted.

"You know, Jake hasn't had an easy life." She smiled and her voice softened. "Don't get me wrong. I don't know what happened between the two of you years ago, and I'm sure it wasn't easy for you. But Jake came home and kept his family together. I think before he found out about Matthew, he was sorry that he'd never had a family of his own."

"Why hasn't he?" Catherine asked.

Ashley lips flattened to a thin line. "It's personal,

so you'll have to ask him. Then maybe you'll understand why he wants so badly to be with Matthew.''

Catherine pondered Ashley's evasive answer. Was there some secret she didn't know about Jake, something that would make him desperate to have possession of his son? Something that would make him threaten to take Matthew from her?

After she finished her coffee, Catherine decided to go outside for a while. She walked over to the corral and stood beside Matthew. She put her arm around him for a hug, then hovered nearby, just wanting a few moments of peace with her son.

Matthew acknowledged his mother with a look that told Catherine he wasn't ready to listen if she was going to try to persuade him to her way of thinking. Catherine kept her distance. In a day or two he wouldn't have a choice. She was going to leave, and no one was going to stop her from taking Matthew with her.

The next day the sun was shining again, and Catherine decided it was now or never. She and Jake had barely spoken the previous day. He'd gone out of his way to avoid her, Catherine thought, which was fine with her. She didn't like the way he made her feel when he looked at her with his brooding expression.

She packed her things in her small bag, then went to look out the window, trying to spot anyone who could thwart her plans. Someone knocked on her door, and Catherine made a beeline for her bag. The door opened about the time that Catherine tossed it to the floor. Guilt tinged her face pink, and she nervously cleared her throat.

''Planning on going somewhere?'' Jake leaned against the doorjamb as his gaze met hers.

Six

Standing beside the bed with the bag at her feet, Catherine paled. "Um, not really. I was going to ask you if you thought the bridge was passable today, though."

"Possibly," he answered, looking as if he didn't believe her. He took a step inside, then was quiet for a few moments. It was obvious that he had something on his mind. Catherine waited nervously for him to speak.

"I guess I was kinda rough on you the other night," he offered, seeming as if he was uncomfortable with admitting as much.

Catherine didn't answer him. She wondered where this was leading. Surely Jake wanted something from her.

"For what it's worth, I'm sorry." He sounded sincere. That didn't mean that he was, she told herself.

She flashed him a curious look, wanting to rattle him as he'd rattled her when he'd come through her door and caught her planning her escape. "For threatening me or for kissing me?"

Jake put a hand on his hip. "Well, for starters, for yelling at you," he replied gruffly. He didn't admit that he shouldn't have kissed her. And he wasn't going to admit that he'd enjoyed it. "I've been thinking, and there's something else I want you to consider." Jake figured if he could avoid taking Catherine to court, it would be better for Matthew. He didn't want to put his son in the middle of a tug-of-war.

The entire situation was difficult for all of them. But the adjustment for Matthew was the most important thing to consider. Catherine had to know that, and Jake was banking on her love for her son to get her to agree to his offer.

"Go on," she encouraged.

"I want Matthew to stay with me for the summer. And you seem to be afraid that if he does, he won't want to come home. Right?"

She nodded at him, her green eyes wary. "Yes."

"I think you should stay at the ranch for the summer, also," Jake suggested. "Then you'd be here with Matthew, and you wouldn't have to worry about what I was telling him or that I was turning him against you."

"For the summer?" Catherine repeated, startled by his proposal. "I couldn't do that. No, that wouldn't work," she said hurriedly, shaking her head.

It hadn't been easy for Jake to offer Catherine this option. Having her live with him was going to be difficult, to say the least. Jake was man enough to admit that he still found her attractive. She was a beautiful woman. Even if he hadn't known her before he would be attracted to her.

He didn't like the feelings she provoked in him, and

having her around to tempt him twenty-four hours a day was going to test his control. But he wanted his son for the summer. This solution was far from perfect, but it would satisfy all concerned.

"It makes sense," he said convincingly. "You'd be right here with Matt. He wouldn't be growing apart from you."

"I understand that part, and I'm not trying to be difficult. It's just that I couldn't possibly leave my home that long," she insisted.

Jake frowned. "Because of this man you're involved with? Shouldn't you put your son first?"

Catherine squared her shoulders. "Douglas has nothing to do with this." It was more the truth than she wanted to admit to Jake. She hadn't given a thought to Douglas the past couple of days, hadn't even called him. All along, in her heart, she'd known that she didn't love him. She'd been foolish to even consider marrying him for Matthew's sake.

"He has a lot to do with this if you're putting him before Matthew."

"I wouldn't do that," she stated firmly.

That statement told Jake a lot about Catherine's relationship with the man. If she was truly in love with him, she would be torn between him and her son. To Jake's knowledge, she hadn't even called the man since she'd been at the ranch.

"What other problem is there?" Jake inquired. "Are you required to work summers with your job?"

"No," Catherine answered honestly. "I could, but I like to have the summers off so I can be with Matthew." Until now she'd looked forward to the end of the school year. She'd hoped to take a summer vacation with her son. There wasn't much chance of that now.

"Then what's stopping you?"

"I don't know, Jake. The whole idea, well, it would be awkward," she stated, shrugging her shoulders.

Jake took a step toward her. "You mean because of the kiss we shared?"

"You kissed me," she reminded him.

"You kissed me back," he returned levelly. "And you enjoyed it."

Catherine didn't deny it. And she knew he knew it was true, even if she didn't admit to it. She flushed to her roots remembering how he'd captured her and held her to him.

"That doesn't mean I wanted you to."

Jake frowned. "If it'll make you feel better, I promise to keep my hands off you while you're here."

Catherine should have drawn comfort from that, but she didn't. That he could turn his feelings on and off so easily disturbed her. She was finding it increasingly hard to keep her distance from Jake. He was an attractive man. He'd been easy to fall in love with.

But he'd hurt her once before. She wasn't going to let him hurt her again. She'd trusted him then, and he'd broken her heart.

"I'd like to talk to Matthew about this." She didn't want to do anything, make any decisions, without first discussing them with her son. "If I say yes, and that's a big if, when do you think you could take us to the airport?"

"I've got some work here at the ranch that's going to keep me busy most of the morning," Jake explained. "I'll be free this afternoon."

"Will we be able to get across the bridge?"

"The bridge won't be a problem," he told her, then

shifted his gaze to the window. "I have a small airplane. I'll fly you home."

Catherine's mouth dropped open. "What?" Irritation swept through her, and she advanced on him. "You mean to tell me that you could have taken me and Matthew home before now?" she demanded.

Jake had the decency to flush just a bit. He put his hands up in defense, as if he thought she was going to hit him.

"No, I'm not saying that—"

"Are you going to stand there and tell me you couldn't have?" Her cheeks were red, her face hot. At that moment, Catherine very much wanted to smack him. To keep from doing so, she rested her hands on her hips. Anger radiated from her.

"It's not as if I knew what the weather was going to do," Jake said in his own defense. "Just because the storms cleared here didn't mean it was okay to fly. I called for a weather report and flying conditions just a few minutes ago."

Catherine made a sound of disgust. "Like you couldn't have done that yesterday," she accused. "Get out of here, Jake."

"Catie—"

"Out!" Her temper simmering, Catherine pointed toward the door.

Jake, apparently not realizing what a mistake he was making, cracked the bare resemblance of a smile. "I'm going." He backed away quickly, then paused at the door. "Let me know when you're ready to go."

"Out!" Catherine shouted, fuming. She put her hands on his back and gave him a shove as he was moving toward the door. Then she slammed it behind him, closing herself in the room.

She couldn't get over how easily she'd accepted the news that she was stuck on the ranch. She'd believed Jake when he said they wouldn't be able to cross the bridge, and all along he had a way to take her and Matthew home.

She had a mind to grab Matthew and go back to her original plan to escape on her own. Damn Jake McCall. He certainly had proved to her that he couldn't be trusted.

And that pretty much meant that she *was* going to have to stay on the ranch for the summer if she allowed Matthew to stay. She wasn't going to trust Jake not to turn her son against her.

Catherine couldn't believe she was in this mess. She had herself to blame, of course. She wished she'd been in tune with Matthew. She should have realized that he was unhappy. And she should have told him the truth about his father a long time ago. Maybe she should have tried a couple of times over the years to contact Jake.

No, this situation was not her fault. It was Jake's, and she was going to keep reminding herself of that. She was going to keep it bottled inside, feed on it and use it as a weapon to keep her wits about her when dealing with Jake.

He'd just proved to her again that he couldn't be trusted.

After a heart-to-heart talk with Matthew, Catherine finally agreed to let him stay on the ranch for the summer, on the condition that she remain there also.

Matthew was ecstatic. He'd even insisted that he didn't want to go home and pack his things. He'd begged Catherine to do it for him, and she'd finally relented and agreed, because it was such an easy thing to do to please her son.

She hadn't, however, thought about the fact that it would mean traveling alone with Jake. She also hadn't thought that it would mean spending a couple of days alone with Jake as she packed.

And most of all, she hadn't realized that she and Jake would be sharing her small condo together.

Alone.

"It really isn't necessary for you to stay," she told Jake as he extended his hand to her. They'd arrived in Lubbock in the afternoon, and Jake had pulled the plane up to a hangar.

Jake sent her an exasperated look. They'd had this conversation before, of course, but she was determined to give it one more try as he opened the door to the plane.

"You're not going to be able to move everything on your own." She'd finally agreed to live on the ranch for the summer. Which meant that for now, Matthew was living with Jake. It appeared to her that Jake didn't want her to get cold feet once she got back home, and the only way he could be sure she wouldn't was to go with her and stay while she packed.

"I can rent a van or something," she said once again, for what seemed like the hundredth time. She was learning that Jake was a very determined man.

Catherine shivered as Jake helped her step down.

"Cold?" he asked.

"A bit," Catherine admitted, her feet finally on firm ground. The recent rain had brought with it a cold front, the temperature dropping lower than normal for this time of year.

Jake shrugged out of his jacket and put it around her, then told her to put her arms in the sleeves. Catherine obeyed and was enveloped by his scent. The coat was still warm from the heat of his body, and a feeling of longing slipped over her.

''Thanks,'' she mumbled, trying not to respond to his nearness or the sensation of desire that pulled at her every time she was close to him.

''No problem.''

Jake got her bag from inside the plane, as well as one of his own. He started them toward the terminal of the airport.

''It'll take me a few minutes to rent a truck,'' he told her, carrying both of their bags.

''My car is already parked here. We can use it,'' she informed him.

''What kind of car do you drive?''

She told him the make and model of her compact car, and he gave a little laugh. ''We'll need something bigger to transport the boxes back to the airport. I figure I'll have to make a few trips. I'm not going to try and fit everything in a small foreign-model car.''

''Are you deliberately trying to bait me?'' Catherine asked, stopping and staring at him.

Jake stared back at her, determined not to smile. He *did* like getting a rise out of her, he realized. ''Not at all. I've just never seen a woman who didn't pack more than she needed,'' he replied, then took her by the arm and steered her in the direction he was heading.

Catherine shook free of his grasp, which earned her a slight grin from Jake. That look, sexy and inviting, fueled her annoyance even as it tripped her heart. She wasn't going to let him push her around.

After Jake rented a large sport utility vehicle, Catherine led the way to her home in her car. Twenty minutes later they both pulled in the driveway, Jake stopping right behind her.

At that moment Catherine would have given anything if she could have avoided going inside. Just thinking about being alone with Jake was enough to unnerve her. Unable to avoid it, she stepped out of her car.

Jake followed her to the door. Catherine lived in a neat neighborhood, with a number of condos matching her own. They were well kept, with shrubs and small flower gardens adorning them.

Catherine used her key to let herself in, then turned to admit Jake before closing the door. She switched a light on, illuminating the small foyer, as well as the living room and small dining area.

It felt strange allowing him into her world, to share her personal space with him. Funny that, after all the years of thinking about him and wondering if she'd ever see him again, she never once imagined him standing in her home.

He was so big that he seemed to fill the room, closing it in, making it seem even smaller than it truly was. Wanting to distance herself, Catherine moved away, then switched on a couple more lights.

"Should I make some coffee?" she asked, doing her best not to look at him. She glanced at her watch, then added, "I imagine you're hungry. I don't have any idea what there is here to eat." She moved about her small kitchen, opening the refrigerator door and examining its contents.

"How about if I go get some hamburgers? While I'm out, I'll try to pick up a few boxes," Jake said. He dropped their bags to the floor, then followed her into the kitchen.

"That's a great idea," Catherine agreed as she continued to study the contents of the refrigerator, thinking it would be a relief to have him out of her home, even if it was for a short while.

Jake hadn't been back to Lubbock since the day he left, and old memories were taunting him. At his home he'd been able to distance himself somewhat from Catie and the feelings she evoked in him.

He was still plenty upset with her, and there was no forgiveness in his heart for her keeping his son from him. There was still the matter of the letter that needed to be cleared up.

The trouble was, Jake hadn't expected to be so attracted to Catie after all these years. He was annoyed at himself for the way he couldn't take his eyes off her backside as she bent over looking in the refrigerator. He resisted the urge to put his hands on her and pull her against him.

She turned around and looked at him then, her eyes connecting with his. Looking uneasy, she walked across the room and brushed by him. "Let me show you where you can sleep tonight."

She started to grab her bag, but Jake got there first and picked them both up. Catherine led the way up the narrow staircase to the second floor. Each room had a separate bath, which she was very thankful for. At least in her home she wouldn't have to share a bathroom with him.

She opened the door to the right, which led to her room. There were beige Priscilla curtains on the windows, and the room was decorated in soft colors of mauve and teal.

"I think it would be best if you slept in here. The bed is bigger, and you'll be more comfortable." Heavens, Catherine thought, Jake sleeping in her bed. Just the thought made her heart turn over with a little thump.

"This is your room," Jake surmised.

"Yes," Catherine answered, turning to look at Jake.

"I'm not sleeping in your bed," he said abruptly. The thought crossed his mind that sleeping with her in her bed would be quite an adventure. He hadn't been with her in nearly thirteen years, hadn't fallen asleep with her in his arms in what felt like a lifetime. He wondered if she still awakened slowly, the way dawn breaks into a new day.

The implications of his words hung between them. Catherine shifted her feet, wondering what he was thinking. Was he remembering the nights they'd slept in each other's arms?

"Oh, but—"

"Matt's bed will be fine," Jake told her, noticing her slight flush and how her green eyes widened. He set her bag on the floor just inside the room.

Catherine started to argue, then changed her mind. She turned around and opened Matthew's door across the hall, not knowing what to expect. His room was fairly neat for an adolescent, his bed unmade, though, and a few of his clothes were strewn across the floor.

Catherine quickly began straightening up, flitting about the room, moving from one place to another to avoid having to turn and face Jake.

"The bed's a double." She indicated the obvious with a toss of her hand.

"It'll be fine," Jake assured her. He came into the room, then dropped his bag on a chair.

"All right, then." Catherine opened the door on the left. "The bathroom is here. There's also one downstairs, just outside the kitchen. I'll get you some clean sheets." She rushed out of the room, then returned with a stack of folded linens in her arms.

She started to strip the bed. As she leaned over, Jake's gaze once again rested on her rear. Her hips moved and swayed as she struggled to get the sheet off one corner of the mattress. Jake nearly groaned watching the process, then damned himself for it.

"I can do that," Jake said curtly, moving beside her and freeing the sheet with one hand. Catherine stepped back as he gathered the sheets up in his hands.

She took them from him. "Um, I'll just go freshen up, then meet you downstairs," she said, backing away. Then she turned and rushed into her own room. She deposited the laundry in the hamper, then ran a brush through her hair. Downstairs a door slammed, and she drew a breath of relief, ready to enjoy a few minutes without Jake's presence.

This was going to be difficult, she told herself. Catherine hadn't expected to feel a sexual attraction to Jake once she saw him again. He'd hurt her, shown he couldn't be trusted. But those things were at complete odds with the feelings he evoked in her.

Catherine turned off her bedroom light, then went downstairs. She decided to use the time she had alone to call Douglas. She played the messages left in her absence. There was one from a co-worker and one from her neighbor, but Douglas hadn't called.

Catherine wasn't really surprised. She dialed his number, wondering if he'd be home. She prayed he was. She didn't want to have this discussion in front of Jake. Douglas surprised her by answering on the first ring.

"It's Catherine," she said, noticing that he seemed rushed.

"Catherine, hi. I was wondering when you'd get back. You just caught me. I was on my way out."

"I arrived home a few minutes ago," she told him. "I'm sorry I didn't call you while I was gone." She hesitated, hating what she had to say over the telephone, but seeing no way out of it. "Do you have a few minutes? I need to talk to you. I'm sorry to do this now, but I'm not going to have time to see you."

Catherine explained about the last two days and what had occurred as briefly as possible. "This is a terrible way to do this, Douglas, but I won't be seeing you anymore. I'm going to be away for the summer. With Matthew. I have to put my son first." She spoke quietly, but her voice was determined. "I'm really sorry to tell you like this."

They talked a little longer, and though Douglas asked a few questions, he didn't seem too disturbed by her declaration or explanation. Catherine was surprised by the relief she felt. Apparently they'd both been willing to settle for less than love. She'd wanted something for herself and her son, so much so that she'd been willing to think that marriage with Douglas would work. She'd foolishly let a comfortable friendship progress too far.

Jake cleared his throat, and Catherine spun around, startled. She hadn't heard him come in. Catherine hurried to end the conversation. She kept her voice quiet but had a feeling that Jake had heard at least part of her conversation. Still, she said nothing to him and ignored the way he glared at her.

They ate the food Jake brought back while packing. She suggested that he should use his judgment on what to bring for Matthew, while she spent time packing her own things. By the end of the night Catherine was exhausted. Jake had come to find her a half dozen times, asking her questions. Together they decided that Matthew would probably want his stereo and computer. Anything else, he would have to live without.

Close to midnight Catherine decided she'd done enough. She'd practically broken her neck to get everything done in one afternoon and evening, trying her best to shorten her stay at her house with Jake. If there was anything else she and Matthew needed, they could buy it. She went downstairs, and Jake was sitting comfortably on her sofa, his long legs stretched out in front of him.

She raised her eyebrows, and he gave her a small grin. Catherine's heart somersaulted. Turning away, she went into the kitchen. "Would you like something to drink?" she asked. "I have sodas and some wine coolers, or if you'd like, I can make some coffee."

"A wine cooler's fine," Jake answered. The last thing he needed was caffeine to keep him awake. What he needed was a cold shower, he decided. Jake had watched Catie all evening as she fretted over what to pack and what to leave. He'd tried to keep his distance as much as possible, but it seemed fate had been working against him. Every time he turned around he'd needed to ask her something.

When he was near her, he wanted to touch her, wanted to kiss her again. She was driving him crazy. He'd promised her he would keep his hands off her, but was having a hard time living up to his word.

He glanced at Catie as she handed him a bottle, then

he diverted his eyes and opened the cool drink. "How long have you lived here?" he asked, curious now to know more about her and his son's past.

Catherine sat in a wooden rocker and sipped her own drink, then set it on the table. "Two years. It took me a while to save up enough money to buy a home." She was proud of what she'd accomplished. It hadn't been easy, but she'd worked hard for everything she had.

Jake frowned, then glanced at the large photo album under one side of the coffee table. He leaned over and picked it up. "Are there pictures of Matthew in here?" He opened it and began scanning the first page.

"Yes." Automatically Catherine got up and moved to sit next to Jake, then smiled as she pointed to a picture of Matthew as a baby. It was natural for Jake to want to see the pictures, and at that moment it felt just as natural for Catherine to share them with him. He was, after all, the father of her child.

Jake flipped the pages slowly, and they shared the memories of their child's life, Catherine talking softly about each picture. Unconsciously she scooted closer to Jake, her bare arm touching his as she pointed to a picture of Matthew as a toddler, taking a bath in bubbles.

Jake was having a difficult time concentrating on the photo album. He was suddenly very aware of Catherine's scent and the warmth of her body gently pressing against his. She leaned closer to reach across the album and talk about a snapshot of Matthew learning to walk. Her hair softly brushed his face, and he could feel her breath on his cheek.

The fact that Jake was determined not to let Catie get under his skin again made little difference as he listened to her talk, her voice sultry and enticing. The sudden urge he had to kiss her was irrational, yet very real and too strong to resist.

Jake turned to ask her a question, and the words died before he could speak. Her mouth was only inches away from his own. His gaze met hers, then dropped to her mouth with silent invitation. Catie didn't move as Jake slowly lowered his mouth onto hers.

He kissed her gently at first, nipping at her lips, tasting her, waiting for her to stop him, to tell him he'd lost his mind. When she didn't, he slipped his tongue farther into her mouth as he cupped her neck and held her lips to his. Fire exploded throughout him as he touched the tip of her tongue.

Catherine tilted her head, angling closer to him, and her hand caressed the back of his head. Jake put his arm around her and pulled her to him, pressing his body against hers.

His mouth left hers, trailing kisses to her ear and down her neck, inflaming the emotions rocketing through him.

"Oh, Jake," Catherine whispered softly, and she pressed a soft kiss beneath his ear. "This shouldn't be happening." Her breathing was labored, her eyes closed.

"No," Jake agreed gravely. His lips nipped hers again, then settled on her mouth, taking it fully beneath his, tasting her again, deeply, a little desperately.

She gave herself in that moment, in that one staggering kiss, and the tangible fire between them became an inferno. Jake cupped her head and chin with both hands, fusing their mouths together, drinking her in. His tongue seared hers, and she moaned, then pressed herself closer to him, her hands gliding along his back.

Jake wanted nothing more at that moment than to be inside her sweet warmth.

"I want you, Catie. Right here, right now," he declared, breathing heavily.

Jake's words exploded in Catherine's mind as he touched her breast, lightly at first, stroking her in a soft, circular rhythm that made her pulse race. Then he filled his hand with her and ran his thumb across her nipple. Aching, it puckered beneath the fabric of her shirt.

Catherine put her hands against Jake's chest, thinking she should stop this insanity. She could feel the heavy thud of his heart beating beneath her palm. Somewhere in the back of her mind the thought that this shouldn't be happening between them disappeared, gone in a moment, replaced by a rapid quickening of need in the deepest core of her.

She clung to him, her hands sliding over his hard muscular shoulders and resting on the corded muscles of his neck. She was unaware of the time or place, oblivious to right or wrong, or if she would regret her actions later. This was Jake, the man she'd loved so deeply once. There was a natural awareness between them that wasn't to be denied.

His hands slid down her body, stroking her, touching her thighs, then returning with sweet torture to her breasts. She reveled in his embrace and the pleasurable memories it provoked.

His mouth devoured hers as he began to unbutton her shirt. Then his hand was inside her blouse, touching her skin, and she arched against it and moaned into his mouth.

Catherine kissed him back hungrily. It had been forever since she'd felt this kind of emotional release, this closeness to another human being.

She'd loved this man once, deeply, and she let herself relive her feelings for him. Touching him, stroking his chest and reaching for the buttons of his shirt. She undid them one by one, then ran her hand over his bare skin.

"Ah, Catie," Jake whispered, then closed his mouth over hers again. In seconds he had her blouse and bra off, then reached for the button to her pants. He slid his hands inside, grasping her buttocks, stroking her, sending a scorching heat racing through her.

"Jake." His lips found her nipple and closed over it, sucking her. She lifted her hips, and his hands slid her pants down.

In a flurry of action, Catherine had his shirt off, and her palms stroked the soft hair on his chest, then slid down his rib cage. He sucked in a hard breath when her hands went to his belt.

"Jeez, Catie, you'd better let me do that," he rasped, then quickly unfastened his belt and slid the zipper of his jeans down.

Catherine felt a moment of hesitation when he moved away to remove his pants and boots, but Jake came to her so quickly, pressing his mouth against hers, touching her breasts, then stroking her intimately as he lowered her to the soft carpet.

He was on top of her then, pressing his body seductively against hers. She could feel him hard and ready as he positioned himself between her thighs. His body began probing hers, gently demanding entry. Then he was inside her. Catherine caught her breath as he invaded her softness.

"Catie…ah, you're so soft, so hot." Jake groaned, a deep growl coming from deep inside his chest. Then he stilled. Panting, he slipped out of her, then lifted himself above her, his gaze seeking hers. "Are you using protection?" he asked, barely able to take a full breath.

Catherine nodded, assuring him she was.

Jake sighed with masculine pleasure as he entered her again, then rocked deeper, his hips provoking hers.

Catherine slid her arms around him, running her hands along his back, her nails sinking into his flesh as she felt her body begin to quiver and tighten.

"Jake, oh, Jake," she murmured, and it sounded like a plea. Molten fire melted her bones, and she felt a huge surge of ecstasy enveloping her. Then Jake was sinking deeper into her, pushing harder and harder. Jake's muscles tightened, and his hands cupped her buttocks as his hips rocked against hers.

And her world exploded.

Seven

Jake's entire body felt as if it weighed a thousand pounds. Making love to Catie had taken everything out of him. All of the pent-up feelings he'd been using as a shield against her and her ability to hurt him disintegrated the moment he'd felt himself inside her. He was sure he must be crushing Catie, but he didn't want to move away from her at that moment. She was soft and warm and pliant beneath him, and with a desperation he wasn't able to understand, he wanted to keep her there.

Then he opened his eyes and saw the photo album. It was open to a page with a picture of Catie standing beside a man. Matthew was in the picture with them. It had been taken at a park. Matt looked to be about eight and wore a baseball uniform. Catie was handing him a bat, and the man was squatting beside Matt, talking to him. That one picture brought it all back home to Jake.

Because of Catie, he'd missed his son's entire childhood. Jake had never had the opportunity to hear Matt's first word, see him crawl or walk, or watch him go off to his first day at school.

How could he have forgotten that Catie had lied to him, that she'd kept his son from him for twelve years? Seeing his son with Catie and this man ripped at his insides. Jake refused to let himself think about how it made him feel to see Catie with another man.

Annoyed with Catie and with his own lack of control, Jake stiffened and rolled away from her. He got to his feet and pulled on his underwear, then his jeans. He should have been the one to teach his son how to bat, how to field a baseball. He should have been there watching his son walk and grow and learn. Seeing his son and Catie together with this *stranger* irritated the hell out of him.

He couldn't bring himself to look at Catie at that moment, but in his peripheral vision he saw her jerky motions as she hurried to dress. She pulled on her flowered blouse and snatched her bra from the floor.

The silence between them was palpable. Jake figured he should say something. He just didn't know *what* to say to her. He shouldn't have let things get so far out of hand, he thought. He shouldn't have kissed her, should never have made love to her. But he hadn't been able to stop himself, and that knowledge left him feeling even more irritated—with his own lack of control as well as with Catie.

He'd asked her about protection because he couldn't admit to her that he was incapable of making her pregnant. His personal life was none of her concern, and he wasn't one to share his innermost feelings. He was glad now that he hadn't slipped up and mentioned it to her. He still didn't trust her, and he wasn't going to give her a weapon to use against him.

Finally, unable to put the uncomfortable conversation off a moment longer, he turned toward her, a frown deepening his brows. "Look, I'm sorry—"

"Stop," she blurted out, interrupting him, her voice eerily calm. She didn't quite meet his gaze. "We're two consenting adults. These things happen. Let's just put this behind us."

Already she was sounding as if she regretted what had happened between them. Jake knew he did. He hadn't meant to complicate matters like this. He wondered if she would back out of coming back to the ranch. If she did, it would be his fault.

Jake didn't know why, but it bothered him that she could so easily explain away their intimacy. He should have felt relieved, but he didn't. He wanted to take her again. Just thinking about her writhing beneath him made him hard.

"Yeah, that's what we'll do," he replied, his tone even as he shrugged into his shirt. He left it unbuttoned. "I guess we should call it a night. We'll be leaving early in the morning, unless you have more packing to do."

Catie shook her head, and still she didn't meet his gaze. "No...no, I'm finished."

A tidal wave of relief washed over Jake. At least she was still planning to come with him to the ranch. He had jeopardized the time he'd been anxiously wanting to spend with his son. Now he was being given another chance. He would have to be more careful around Catie.

"I'll turn in, then."

Catie made no comment, so Jake walked toward the staircase. He hesitated, then climbed the stairs.

Catherine watched Jake's back as he ascended the staircase. There was no way she would let him know how much he'd hurt her. The tension in her body coiled as he disappeared and she heard the door to her son's room open. It wasn't until he closed the door behind him that she dropped onto the sofa. She wrapped her arms around herself and rocked back and forth.

She was *not* going to let herself fall in love with Jake again. He'd hurt her terribly once. She'd be a fool to let him hurt her like that again.

She couldn't believe that she'd so easily succumbed to Jake's sexual advances. Of course when they'd been together years ago their bodies had been very attuned to each other. Catherine figured that for a few moments she'd allowed herself to go back in time.

What had happened between her and Jake wasn't real. They'd both been carried away with memories of a period when they'd laughed and loved.

Her gaze fell to the photo album spread open on the floor and the pictures of Matthew playing Little League. So that was it, she thought. That was all it took for Jake to pull away from her and withdraw within himself.

He still blamed her, when it was his own fault for not knowing about his son. Whether he believed it or not, she'd tried several times to contact him. In the morning she'd show him the letter.

She took a deep breath, gathered herself together, then stood and switched off the lights in the room. Slowly she walked up the stairs to her bedroom. Her body was slightly sore, and would probably be more so in the morning.

Trying to ease the tension pulling at her, she took a hot bath. Long afterward she lay between cool sheets, alone in her room with thoughts of Jake sleeping nearby. It was well into the night before she fell asleep.

The ride to the airport was filled with tension, and Catherine knew Jake felt it, too. During their preparations to leave, they had barely spoken to each other. Jake had refused breakfast and made a trip to load packages on the plane. Catherine had used the time to toss perishables in the trash and ready her condo for her absence.

Jake loaded the truck with the last of the boxes while Catie made arrangements with a neighbor to keep an eye on things for her. She'd mentioned driving her car to Jake's, but he'd insisted she wouldn't need it. He explained that there were several ranch vehicles, and she could have free use of any of them whenever she needed.

Catherine had been relieved just to get on the road and out of her home. Every time she looked at the living room floor, she remembered Jake making love to her there. Was she never going to learn?

Once at the airport Jake transferred the last of the boxes to the airplane. After returning the truck he'd rented, he did a final check on the plane before they took off.

Catherine had waited by the plane for him to finish. She hesitated only a fraction of a moment when Jake offered her his hand to help her on board. Her heartbeat quickened as she felt his big hand grasp hers. With his other hand he touched the small of her back, giving her support, and Catherine felt her knees go weak.

She silently admonished herself for her reaction to him as she took a seat in the plane and Jake climbed in and started it.

She needed to physically and emotionally distance herself from Jake, but that was going to be hard to accomplish, since they were now on their way to his ranch where she'd agreed to live for the entire summer. She would have backed out if she hadn't already made promises to her son.

Surely Jake had a lot of responsibilities at the ranch, and they wouldn't be tripping over each other. Of course there were going to be times when they'd be together. At least then there would be other people around them.

Catherine would give staying at the ranch a fair chance since it was so important to Matthew. She wasn't doing it for Jake, although she knew he had the power to make life miserable for her by trying to get custody of Matthew.

Catherine couldn't let it come to that. After spending the summer with Matthew she hoped Jake would be reasonable about working out visitation arrangements. And if it did come down to a court battle, it would look good on her part that she'd agreed to let father and son have the summer together.

Catherine was relieved when they finally approached the ranch. She and Jake hadn't made much conversation on the trip. Obviously he was regretting their intimacy as much as she was. Well, that was okay with her. It let her know where he stood. She was all for being polite and distant with Jake. She just hoped her heart was going to follow the rules.

Jake radioed ahead and let Ryder know they were near arrival. Matthew was with Ryder when he drove out to meet them, and it was evident that her son had already established a kinship with his uncle.

Matthew ran to greet her and Jake, his eyes brilliant with excitement as he chatted on and on about his activities since they'd been gone. Catherine doubted that her son had even missed her. She was amazed by the change in his disposition. He acted as if feeding cattle was as interesting and fun as the games on his computer.

"Hey, son," Jake said, smiling as he ruffled the young boy's hair. "Sounds like you've been learning a lot about the ranch while we were gone." Catherine felt her heart turn over at the way Matthew grinned up at him, he looked so happy. It was obvious he was already taking to the ranch and his new family.

"Uncle Ryder let me ride some more today," he told them, his voice high-pitched with excitement.

Jake began unloading the cargo. He handed Matthew a box to carry. With everyone helping, it wasn't too long before everything they'd brought was transferred to the house and into the two bedrooms Catherine and Matthew would use for the summer.

Finally left alone, Catherine stood in the middle of her room, listening to the sounds coming from the adjoining bathroom. Good heavens, how could she have forgotten that she was going to be sharing a bathroom with Jake? So much for keeping her distance, she thought.

She surveyed the boxes of clothing she'd brought. Since Ryder no longer used the room, there was plenty of space for her things. She'd given Matthew orders to unpack his belongings before he could go outside again. She thought she might as well get hers done also.

As she began to fill the dresser drawers, the commitment she'd made to stay the summer with Jake and his family hit her. It had been a long time since Catherine had felt part of a family. She hadn't talked to her parents or sisters since she'd left school. Catherine had accepted the fact that she'd let her parents down and they didn't want anything to do with her.

Deep down inside, though, she still felt an enormous emptiness when she thought about her two younger sisters. They would be adults now. For years after she'd left, she'd hoped to see them again one day.

Now she was here with this big, happy family. Matthew was settling in nicely, enjoying the attention and affection of new aunts, uncle and cousins. But Catherine couldn't help feeling out of place. The strain between her and Jake wasn't going to help things.

She finished unpacking the last box, then tossed it aside. Glancing at the clock, she realized it was nearly time to prepare dinner. Perhaps she could offer to help.

Catherine had been tossing an idea around in her head since she'd agreed to stay for the summer. She wasn't about to sit around for weeks and not contribute in some way for her keep.

She headed out of her room and went looking for Ashley. Ryder's wife was really nice and Catherine liked her a lot already. She found her in the den, playing with her twins.

"Hi," Catherine said, walking into the room.

Ashley looked up from where she was sitting on the floor with the two toddlers. "Catherine, hi." She smiled, then grabbed Michelle's hand just before she could throw a small wooden block at her sister.

"I was wondering if I could talk to you—sometime when you're not too busy," she added, then realized how ridiculous that sounded. What expectant mother with twins wouldn't be busy all the time?

"Sure." Ashley quickly got to her feet, though she leaned backward a moment and stretched. Michelle and Melissa both crawled over and tugged on her legs. "I was just about to feed these two. Wanna help?"

Catherine gave her an answering smile. "I'd love to," she replied.

"Great!" Ashley scooped up Michelle. "Grab Melissa, will you?" she asked, starting from the room.

"You don't breast-feed?" Catherine followed Ashley to the kitchen.

Ashley shook her head. "I did for a while, but I stopped after I became pregnant. I was just so exhausted. Still am, for that matter."

Catherine smiled. "You'd never know it," she commented as she took a seat.

"By the end of the day I can barely hold my eyes open," Ashley confessed. She prepared the bottles for the babies, then handed one to Catherine before sitting with Michelle still in her arms. "But I'm lucky. Ryder's a great father, and his family has practically adopted me."

Ashley gave Catherine a curious look and went on. "You know it was really hard for me at first. I wasn't sure about living here. I didn't know anyone, and I felt really insecure. But the McCalls are unbelievably close, and they welcomed me into their fold without hesitation."

Catherine held the bottle to Melissa's tiny mouth. She grabbed hold of the nipple and sucked. "That's sort of how I feel, though my stay isn't permanent."

She looked contrite for a moment. "I'm sorry. I didn't mean that you or anyone else has made me uncomfortable."

Ashley gave Catherine a warm smile. "No offense taken. I can see why we'd be a bit overwhelming."

After a few minutes Catherine propped Melissa on her shoulder and patted her back. The baby offered up a small burp. "I don't have any family to speak of, but not living in my home feels strange."

"Are you sure it isn't that you're living so close to Jake now?" Ashley boldly asked. "I get the feeling that all is not quite well between you two. He was awfully quiet when he came through here a little while ago, and when I asked about you, he just grunted something unintelligible."

Ashley was very astute, Catherine thought. "We did have a couple of clashes while we were gone," she confessed without going into details. "I thought about not coming, but it was so important to Matthew. I figured I could at least give it a try."

Melissa finished the last of her bottled milk, and Catherine used a cloth to clean her bow-shaped mouth. "I was thinking, though, that I'll go crazy if I don't have something to do this summer." Her gaze met Ashley's. "I don't want to get in the way or anything, but how would you feel if I helped with the house while I'm here instead of having someone come in?"

Ashley was pleased by the suggestion. "Are you sure you want to?"

Catherine nodded. "I need to do something, and I'd feel as if I was earning my stay, so to speak," she explained.

"Well, I think it's a great idea, because I'd rather not have a stranger come in."

Catherine thought that was an odd statement, since she was virtually a stranger to Ashley.

"I know what you're thinking, and you're no longer a stranger in this house. Matthew is Jake's child. You're Matthew's mother. That makes you part of this family," she explained, as if it was simply that easy to rationalize.

Catherine felt an overwhelming sense of longing. She *wished* at that moment that she was truly a part of this loving family. "That's really nice of you to say."

Ashley grinned. "I mean it." She finished feeding Michelle, then frowned at Catherine. "I'm not sure how Jake will accept this idea, though."

Catherine squared her shoulders. "Jake will have to live with it. I made a concession in coming here. If you have no problem with my help, why should he?"

Ashley grinned. "Why, indeed?" she repeated, thinking Jake had finally met his match. She was going to enjoy seeing him go toe-to-toe with Catherine. "Well, I guess I'd better get these two down for a nap."

"Let me help," Catherine insisted, following Ashley out of the room. She'd gotten over one hurdle talking to Ashley. Now all she had to do was talk to Jake.

Catherine had silently practiced her speech a couple of times as she helped with preparing the meal. She had planned to confront Jake with her idea after dinner. She hadn't figured on Ashley announcing it to everyone while they were eating.

As soon as Ashley had mentioned Catherine's "kind" offer, Jake's gaze shot to Catherine's. "That's not necessary," he stated in that controlling tone of his.

"Actually, it is necessary for you to have someone

come in to help out,'' Catherine informed him. ''Why shouldn't it be me?''

Jake grunted his disapproval. ''Because you're a guest,'' he insisted. ''Guests don't do housework and laundry.'' He stared back at Catherine, his eyes hard and unyielding.

''That's ridiculous, Jake,'' Ashley gently admonished her brother-in-law. ''Catherine's no more a guest than I was when I came here, and you accepted the fact that I wanted to work.''

Her reminder fell on deaf ears. ''That was different.'' His expression softened a bit when he glanced at Ashley.

A small smile played on her lips. ''I don't see how.'' She looked at Ryder, who had been quiet to this point. ''Do you, honey?''

''Nope, darlin', I don't,'' he agreed. He gave his older brother a sharp look, obviously enjoying his disgruntled expression. ''Unless you can explain it to us,'' he added, fighting back a grin.

Catherine wasn't exactly sure what was happening. Obviously, she had the support of Jake's sibling and his wife. She just wasn't sure why.

''I think it's a great idea,'' Lynn said, pointing her fork at Jake as she spoke. ''I can understand why Catherine doesn't want to sit around and twiddle her thumbs.''

Jake could see that he was totally outnumbered and wasn't going to stand a chance of getting out of this. He wasn't sure why he didn't want Catie cleaning the house or doing laundry, except that it seemed like an awfully personal thing to be doing for them.

For him.

"Mom's a cleaning fanatic," Matthew chimed in. "She'll probably drive you all crazy."

"Matthew!" Catherine gasped. Her son gave her a knowing look, and she returned a censuring one.

"You'll get paid, then," Jake said by way of conceding.

"I will not," Catherine stated firmly.

"You will or you won't be doing the work," he returned flatly, the decision already made in his mind.

"You can't make me take money," Catherine replied, her voice just as determined as Jake's.

Jake's jaw tightened. He'd been glad to have work to do away from the house after they'd returned from Lubbock. He'd managed to avoid Catie until dinnertime. Now he was having to look directly at her, and it was driving him crazy. He felt an overwhelming urge to drag her from the table and kiss her senseless. Staying away from Catie was going to be his undoing.

He glanced at his son who was taking in the entire conversation. The last thing he wanted was to upset Matthew.

"Let's discuss this outside," he suggested to Catie, shoving back his chair so abruptly that it squeaked across the floor.

Catherine shot him a hard look. "Let's," she agreed, getting out of her seat and following him out the back door.

The June evening had turned slightly cool, but the sky was clear and lit with stars easily seen without the intrusion of city lights. Catherine couldn't get over how beautiful it was. She rarely had the opportunity to leave the city. She was going to spend a lot of time at night watching the sky.

She turned to face Jake, her heart skipping a beat as

she realized that he was standing close beside her. Barely able to breathe, she took a small step away from him. "I really don't want to argue with you about this, Jake," she insisted, and her voice suddenly sounded husky. "I want something to do this summer."

Jake's gaze fell on Catherine's face, and all he could think about was kissing her. He wondered how he could be so angry with her and still want to make love to her.

"I don't want you keeping house for us," he stated tersely, his emotions in turmoil.

Catherine's gaze connected with his, her eyes fiery. "And everything has to be your way, is that it?" she demanded. Catherine saw his jaw tighten a fraction. Jake was used to making decisions. Well, she was going to get her way this time.

"I've changed my entire summer plans to stay here with Matthew. Whether you believe it or not, I did that for you as well as for him. I can't sit here all summer long with nothing to do. Now, whether you like it or not, I *am* going to help out around here!"

Finished with her diatribe, Catie was breathing heavily. Jake's gaze took in all of her. Her breasts were rising and falling rapidly with every breath she took, straining against the pale-blue blouse she wore. Her eyes flashed hotly, and her hands rested on her slim hips.

Jake had a feeling he was in deep trouble. He wanted nothing more at the moment than to drag her to the ground and strip her clothes off. He had to fight the desire to show her exactly what she was doing to him.

Grating his teeth, he grunted, "Have it your way."

Catherine frowned. "What?"

Frustrated, Jake swore. "You heard me. Do whatever you want."

A smile caught on Catherine's lips. She hadn't expected him to give in without more of a fight. "Hmm," she taunted. "No more arguments?" She was surprised that he'd given in so easily, and she was enjoying her triumph. She couldn't help flaunting her victory just a little.

Jake stared at her. "Don't push me, Catie," he growled, not at all happy that he was giving in to her.

Catherine grinned up at him. "Or what? What's wrong, Jake? Are you not used to losing, or is it that you don't like losing to me?" She licked her lips, and her eyes lit with teasing.

Jake stared at her, and he wanted to take her down a notch or two. He knew the best way to do that and to satisfy his own itch.

"Or this," he grumbled.

He snaked his hand around her neck and pulled her forward with enough force to press her body flat against his. Her startled cry caused her mouth to open, and Jake took full advantage of it. He clamped his mouth over hers and smothered the sound of protest that automatically came from her.

Catherine's hands pressed hard against Jake's chest. His free arm came around her like a band of steel, molding her against him. The onslaught of his kiss stunned her and left her unable to react, other than to moan with pleasure as his tongue found hers.

Never taking his mouth from hers, Jake deepened the kiss, his lips hard and demanding, and Catherine responded without giving thought as to why she shouldn't. All sense of reality slipped away from her when Jake's hand slipped up her rib cage and touched her breast.

Her nipples hardened, aching for his touch, and she moved against him, then was immediately aware of his arousal. Before she could react, Jake broke off the kiss and firmly pushed her away from him.

"Be careful in the future not to push me too far," he warned her, trying to get his own breathing under control. "Next time I may not stop, and believe me, you won't want me to."

He turned abruptly and left Catherine standing there staring at his retreating back. She lifted her hand to her lips, swollen now from his kisses. The memory of the taste of him, of how it felt to be pressed against him, rushed over her.

Catherine knew that she was fighting a losing battle. Her heart was in danger, and there was little she could do to protect it when Jake McCall was around.

Eight

The first order of business the next day, Jake had decided, was to find out what had prompted Frank Davis to send a letter to Catie on Jake's behalf. They'd gone into Crockett, which was why he and Catie were waiting in the law offices of Rand Jensen. He'd bought Frank's practice and assumed responsibility for Frank's clientele, and Jake had used Rand's services often enough to be on a first-name basis with his paralegal.

Jake glanced at Catie, who was seated across from him. She'd shown him Frank Davis's letter the morning they were leaving Lubbock to return to the ranch. At that time they'd been barely speaking, so Jake hadn't discussed it with her. But he'd thought about it a lot since then.

It had been brief and to the point, only a couple of sentences to inform the recipient that she'd contacted the wrong person. Jake understood why Catie had been so hurt, but it wasn't as if it was *his* fault. He hadn't known a thing about it. To Jake's way of thinking it didn't excuse what she'd done.

"Come on in, Jake."

Jake looked up and nodded at Peggy Lewis. "Thanks, Peg," Jake said, then waited for Catie to precede him. Peggy led them to a conference room where a stack of folders was sitting neatly on a small, rectangular conference table.

"Make yourselves at home. The files you wanted to see are right there," she said, pointing to the stack. She smiled pleasantly, then promptly left them alone.

Jake grimaced as he and Catie took a seat. He wasn't sure what they would find. He reached for the folders and glanced over them, then chose one to look at. It was labeled Correspondence, and contained a thick stack of papers. Jake moved the folder so Catie could see it, also, which brought him close enough to her to smell her perfume. He had to resist the urge to touch her. Steeling himself, he turned his attention to the letters.

It took a few minutes because the file was in disarray. Frank's wife had been his secretary, and she'd only worked half a day. Jake grunted when he realized they would have to search through the entire file, and even then there was a chance that they wouldn't find any answers.

About halfway through, Jake came upon a copy of the letter that was sent to Catie, with her letter attached. He flipped the pages, then reread the words Catie had written him all those years ago. The anguish she'd felt was apparent. Though she hadn't mentioned the baby, she had practically pleaded with Jake to call her.

"I don't understand," Jake murmured, shaking his

head. Why hadn't Frank asked him about this before he'd answered Catie?

"What?"

"Why would Frank send you that letter?" he asked aloud. He turned the pages over, searching for some kind of answer, but there wasn't even a clue. Frustrated, Jake continued going through the stack. Just as he was about to give up, he spotted a small note written on a scrap of pink paper.

"Damn." Jake studied it, and a distant memory tugged at his mind.

"What?" Catherine asked.

Jake leaned closer to her. "Look at this." He handed her the paper. The date on it was a week after Catie's letter had arrived at Frank's office, and there was a notation that he'd talked with Jake.

"It says, 'Kathleen.'"

Jake swore again, and his lips thinned. "I vaguely remember one day when Frank came out to the ranch on some business. He'd been in a hurry. Just as he was leaving, he asked me if I knew a Kathleen. He said that he'd gotten a letter from someone named Kathleen, but at the time he couldn't recall a last name." Jake sighed heavily. "He never mentioned it again after that, and I never gave it any more thought."

"Oh, Jake." Catie touched his arm.

"Frank must have thought he'd asked me about the right person, then sent a letter to you." He turned and looked into Catherine's green eyes. "I'm sorry, Catie. I never made the connection."

Catherine wanted to cry, and sniffed back the tears threatening to spill from her eyes. So many years. So many hurtful, agonizing years. All because one man made a mistake. Even if she and Jake had never gotten back together, Matthew would have had a chance to know his father. She would have *wanted* him to.

"Don't cry," Jake said, then touched her cheek with the pad of his thumb.

Jake's breath whispered over her mouth, and Catherine's breath caught. She licked her lips, then blinked. A tear slipped from the inner corner of her eye, then slid down her cheek.

"All because of a simple mistake," she murmured sorrowfully.

Jake nodded thoughtfully. "At least the mystery is solved. You know, it's not as if Frank did it on purpose."

Catie moved away, breaking contact with Jake. In essence he was reminding her that she'd purposefully kept Matthew from him. But she didn't apologize. She had thought that Jake didn't want to hear from her. And if he'd loved her the way he'd professed, he would have called her, she silently reasoned. How could he blame her, when he was guilty of the same thing?

Catherine had never been on a horse in all her life. From the looks of things, that probably wasn't going to change. So what if she'd grown up in Texas? Not *everyone* in Texas knew how to ride a horse. She stared at the big gray mare that Ryder had brought out from the barn, watching from a distance as Jake's brother tossed a worn saddle on her back.

Reading her uneasy manner, Ryder patted the horse along her neck. "This is Flo. She's real gentle," he assured Catherine in that charming tone of his.

Looking from Ryder to the horse, Catherine wasn't so sure. She didn't want Ryder to think that she didn't trust his judgment, but something inside her resisted the idea of sitting on the animal. "I don't know about this," she confessed shakily.

"Don't worry, darlin'. Flo will do all the work." He gave Catherine a reassuring grin, his mustache turning slightly upward. "She's done this before, you know. All you have to do is get on, and she'll do the rest."

When Ryder grinned like that, Catherine knew why Ashley had fallen in love with him. He had a magnetism like no other man Catherine had known. Ashley was a lucky woman.

But no matter what Ryder said, Flo was a big animal and a bit scary, too. "I don't see why it's so important for me to learn to ride a horse," Catherine said, sounding as anxious as she felt.

Ryder gave her a patient look. "You've been here several weeks and you're already antsy. You've cleaned the house until it's spotless. Ashley told me I'd better get you outside before you go crazy. The best way to deal with excess energy is to get out in the summer sunshine."

Fluttering her eyes, Catherine replied, "Shopping works, too."

Ryder chuckled. "C'mon. Riding a horse can be fun. Just give it a chance."

Catherine wasn't so sure about that. Ryder had insisted that Flo was gentle, easy on beginners. He didn't seem the type to lie, but she had a distrustful nature. She put her foot inside the stirrup and jumped. Flo did a little sidestep, then whinnied.

Exasperated, Catherine stepped back and took a breath. "Maybe I should try another time."

"Catherine, you can do this," Ryder encouraged. "C'mon, I'll help you." He instructed her to put her foot in the stirrup, then when she jumped, he put his hand under her backside and gave her a push upward. Catherine landed in the saddle, her hands grasping the saddle horn as she bent over.

"Don't you have something else to do?" a hard voice questioned, interrupting them. Jake stared at Ryder, his hands on his hips.

Ryder's palm rested along Catherine's backside. He held the reins in his other hand. He'd seen his brother approaching out of the corner of his eye. Ignoring the harsh tone of Jake's voice, Ryder turned his back to him.

"I thought it was about time Catherine learned to ride," he offered, giving Catherine a smile and a wink.

"I thought *you* were going out to the south pasture to check the fencing today," Jake reminded his younger brother. He glanced at Ryder's hand again and didn't think it was appropriate for him to be touching Catie so intimately.

Very slowly Ryder turned to face his brother. "The last time I checked, I was pretty much my own boss."

"I didn't say you weren't," Jake replied stiffly.

"Look," Catherine said, interrupting them, "I'm not too fond of this idea, anyway. Why don't I just—"

Ryder touched Catherine's thigh, then took note of the way Jake chewed at the inside of his mouth. "Stay put, darlin'," he said when she made as if to dismount. Without a fraction of hesitation, he confronted his brother with a sharp look.

"Catherine's been working hard for the past few weeks. She cleans the house, does tons of laundry and is one of the best damn cooks Texas can claim. She deserves some time off to relax."

"No one's sayin' she doesn't," Jake countered, glaring at them both.

"Well, she admitted at dinner last night that she didn't know anything about riding, and you didn't exactly jump up and volunteer to teach her." There was an accusation in his tone.

That was true enough, Jake thought. He'd been working with Matthew daily, wanting his son to learn how to handle a horse on his own. He was proud of Matt's progress, too, though he hadn't yet allowed him to ride alone.

"I'll take over now," Jake stated, and he sounded as if it was going to kill him to do so.

Jake had tried his best to stay away from Catie because he was all too aware of his attraction to her. He hadn't *wanted* to teach her to ride until he walked up and saw his brother instructing her. They looked just a little too friendly. Not that Jake thought Ryder would ever betray Ashley, but Catie was a beautiful woman who could turn any man's head.

Ryder gave Jake a sharp look. "With that kind of attitude, Catherine might not want your help," he commented.

"I don't have an *attitude*," Jake countered.

Ryder's hand went to his hip. "Sure could've fooled me."

Catherine was sure she looked as uncomfortable as she felt. The last thing she wanted was to make Jake feel as if he was being forced to teach her to ride. And she sure didn't want to be alone with him. "Let's not worry about it right now," she insisted, squirming in her seat. "I'm not really ready for this, anyway."

Ryder patted her thigh again, then handed the reins to Jake. "Don't be silly, darlin'. You're goin' to have a ball." Grinning, he stepped back. "She's all yours," he said to his brother. Giving Catherine one of his warmest smiles, he added, "You're in good hands."

Catherine didn't doubt that. Jake's hands, as she well knew, were all too capable in more ways than one. He checked the saddle and adjusted it a bit, her heart thumping a little harder as he nudged her leg with his arm.

"Jake, we don't have to do this," she insisted, self-conscious from being turned over to him.

He frowned at her. "Do you think I can't teach you to ride?" he demanded, giving her that patently challenging look of his.

"I'm not saying that at all!" Catherine gritted her teeth, trying to think of some way to get out of this.

"Maybe you're afraid to be alone with me."

His blunt statement silenced Catherine. She swallowed hard, trying to find her voice. "That's ridiculous. Why would I be?" she finally replied, bravely leveling him with a stare.

Jake didn't answer. He just turned away from her, and Catherine had no idea what he was thinking. "Hold on," he instructed, then moved forward, leading the horse with the reins.

Catherine fell forward and grabbed at anything to keep from falling. Flo did another little sidestep and lifted her head, shaking her thick mane. Jake almost laughed at Catherine's expression of fear, but appeared to check himself at the last minute.

"Loosen up a little," he instructed, giving the horse a reassuring pat. "You're scaring Flo and making her nervous."

"*I'm* making *her* nervous?" Catherine countered, breathless. "She's the one making me nervous."

Jake studied the situation. "Well, she wouldn't if

you'd stop hanging on to the saddle horn as if you were glued to it.''

The tension along Catherine's spine mounted as she contemplated Jake's words. There was no way she was loosening her grip. She tried to straighten her back so it would appear that she was more at ease.

Apparently she didn't fool Flo or Jake a bit. The horse that Ryder insisted was *gentle* seemed uneasy and not at all worthy of Catherine's trust. Jake just glared at her.

"Here," Jake said. He brought the horse to a halt, then turned around and stood beside her. "Scoot up in the saddle.''

Before she knew what he meant to do, he moved her foot out of the stirrup. Then he swiftly mounted the horse and slid behind Catherine, which molded her bottom intimately against him.

His arms came around her, and he pried her fingers from the saddle. "I've got you," he said, holding her tight about the waist. "You need to loosen up a bit. Flo won't have any problem with you riding her as long as she thinks you know what you're doing.''

"Well, I *don't* know what I'm doing," Catherine reminded him tightly. "And I don't think your being up here with me is going to fool her.''

Jake chuckled, then clicked his tongue and jabbed the horse lightly with his heels. Flo responded immediately and moved forward. Instinct made Catherine squeal, but Jake whispered in her ear to take a breath.

Catherine wished she *could* get a deep breath. This was so much more than she'd bargained for when she'd confessed at dinner that she'd never learned to ride a horse. Her breath dammed up inside her, and she knew it didn't have anything to do with riding Flo.

Jake took her hands in his, then gave her the reins, instructing her on how to guide the horse. They rode around in big circles.

"You're still too uptight," Jake commented. "Relax."

Catherine wondered how she was supposed to accomplish that with Jake whispering in her ear, his breath fanning her cheek. Her heart constricted, and the air she'd sucked in got trapped somewhere inside her lungs.

Jake's warm body was wrapped around hers, and Catherine felt as if she was going to melt against him if she relaxed even a fraction. What she wanted more than anything was to be off the horse and out of Jake's arms. But there was no way she was going to let Jake know how he made her feel.

Since the night after dinner when he'd kissed her, he'd done his best to steer clear of her. For the most part Catherine saw him only at meals. He might be physically attracted to her, but he seemed to not want to explore his feelings.

Well, Catherine wasn't stupid. If Jake felt regretful about the night they'd made love, then so did she. It *had* been stupid of her to let it happen. The trouble was, she admitted to herself, she couldn't seem to forget how easily she'd come apart when he kissed her...or how much she still wanted him to.

"Hey, Mom!" Matthew came running up to them, his green eyes big and round. "Wow, you're learning to ride, too!" he exclaimed.

Catherine tried to give her son a confident grin as Jake slowly brought the horse to a stop. She'd been about to let Jake know that she'd changed her mind, that she wasn't really interested in learning to ride.

Now, with the way Matthew was gazing up at her, his eyes aglow, she had to rethink her decision. She didn't want to disappoint him. Forcing a smile, she said, "I'm giving it a try."

Matthew grinned. "Dad says anyone can learn to ride."

Catherine's stomach somersaulted. Matthew had called Jake *Dad*. Twisting around, she looked at Jake, and his gaze collided with hers.

"He asked me this morning if he could call me Dad," Jake told her, his tone thick with emotion.

"Oh, Jake," Catherine said on a whisper, her voice cracking. Tears stung her eyes. Clearly, Matthew's request had taken his father by surprise. She could see how much it meant to him, and her insides melted a little. A tearful smile wavered on her lips.

Jake's gaze fell to her mouth, then traveled back up to her eyes. All of his good intentions about not getting involved with Catie disappeared as he remembered the way she tasted when they'd made love. Everything and everyone around them ceased to exist.

Without even thinking about it, Jake bent his head in her direction. Flo chose that moment to whinny and move, breaking Jake's gaze with Catherine's. Jake grabbed the reins and gentled the horse.

What an idiot, he admonished himself. Wanting Catie was driving him crazy. Without preamble, he dismounted.

"That's enough for today," he stated gruffly. He slid Catherine's foot into the stirrup, then motioned for her to get off the horse. Catherine swung her leg over the side of Flo and slid down, aware of Jake's strong hands on her waist. When she had sure footing, he let her go. She didn't look at him.

"It's getting late. I'd better go see about helping with dinner," she said, looking down and dusting her jeans with her hands. She couldn't bring herself to look at Jake, couldn't bear to let him see how he affected her. "Thanks," she offered, then called to Matthew. "Come on in and wash up."

Jake watched Catherine walk away, admiring the gentle sway of her hips. He thought about having made love to her after all the years they'd been apart, and his body tightened with consuming lust. He wanted to slide into her again, to feel her heat, to see her come apart in his arms.

He'd been with his share of women over the years, but after Maxine he'd never been tempted to form a permanent, lasting relationship with any of them. Only once had he felt like that—a long time ago with Catie.

And she'd lied to you, his mind taunted. *She kept your son a secret, kept him from you.*

Secrets.

Jake couldn't seem to let her deceit go. Everyone important to him had hurt him. His father. Maxine.

Now Catie. Regardless of the letter his lawyer had sent, she should have tried to contact Jake again.

He couldn't allow himself the luxury of trusting Catie. He had too much to lose. Desiring her was one thing. He could handle wanting her. But he couldn't take a chance on getting his heart broken.

Despite his reasoning, Jake watched her disappear into the house, and all he could think about was how much he wanted her.

Damn, he was a fool.

Nine

Catherine wasn't prepared for what was coming. She'd tried and said everything she could think of to get out of it. After that first day, she had assumed that Jake wouldn't continue trying to teach her to ride.

She'd been dead wrong. Ryder had brought it up at dinner the very evening of her first lesson, asking how it went, egging his brother on by declaring that he could teach Catherine to ride if Jake couldn't.

Jake seemed determined not to let Ryder get the best of him. He stated that he was expecting to continue with her lessons each day, just as he was with Matthew's.

After a few weeks Catherine felt as if she was beginning to get the hang of riding. Flo didn't seem nearly as nervous, which made Catherine more at ease, and the two of them appeared to be less leery of each other.

Today was supposedly Catherine's big moment. She groaned as she left the safety of her room and headed toward the front door. Okay, so maybe she was dreading being alone with Jake more than she was reluctant about riding Flo. After all, she and the horse had apparently made peace with each other.

Not Catherine and Jake. There was an unspoken awareness between them that seemed to spark every moment they came into contact with each other. Catherine had endured being alone with Jake without giving him any hints that she was in danger of falling in love with him again.

She wasn't sure how much longer she could go on being near him. She didn't think the attraction she felt was one-sided. The smoldering looks Jake gave her now and then made her shiver with need. He'd almost kissed her the day he'd started teaching her to ride. Catherine had started wondering *when* he would kiss her again.

She crossed the yard and went into the barn. The acrid smells of hay and horses hit her as she walked inside, and she let her eyes adjust to the shadows of the structure. Jake had taught her to saddle Flo, though Catherine still had trouble lifting the heavy saddle on her own.

Russ Logan was in the barn, and she greeted him as she approached Flo's stall. As Catherine led the horse outside, he offered to get the saddle for her, and for that Catherine was grateful. He was a quiet man who kept to himself most of the time, though from comments she'd heard, he was well liked by most everyone who lived on the ranch. And heavens, he was handsome in a rugged, cowboy-of-the-West sort of way.

His eyes seemed to miss nothing. He didn't talk very

much, which didn't exactly encourage idle conversation. Catherine sensed there was a lot to this man, only he wasn't letting anyone close enough to discover much about him.

As Russ lifted the saddle to Flo's back, Catherine raised her hand to shade her eyes from the hot sun so she could study him. Though he seemed nice enough, she was all too aware of his fiery altercations with Lynn. Catherine shook her head thoughtfully. As far as Jake's sister was concerned, Russ Logan was pigheaded and cantankerous. Catherine could see none of those traits in the good-looking, quiet man standing before her.

He turned toward her, and Catherine smiled. "Thanks, Russ."

"No problem, ma'am." Russ nodded, his gaze locking briefly with hers before breaking contact.

Catherine went about the task of securing the saddle, patting Flo and talking quietly to her. She put her hand in her pocket and pulled out a piece of carrot to offer the horse.

"Okay, you can do this," Catherine whispered to herself when Russ was out of hearing distance. Jake was expecting her to ride out with him today. He would be showing up at any moment, and she was determined to appear calm and sure of herself, despite the reservations attacking her at the moment.

Actually she and Flo had gotten along quite well over the past few weeks that Catherine's lessons had taken place. Jake had even complimented her several times.

Catherine put her foot in the stirrup and took a deep breath. She mounted Flo without difficulty, then let out a puff of air. She had wanted to show Jake that she was capable of mastering riding, and she'd worked hard to keep up with Matthew. Leaning forward, she patted Flo affectionately. As she sat up, she caught sight of Jake riding into the yard on his brown roan.

Her heart skipped a beat. She sat straighter, wishing he didn't have the power to make her heart ache so.

He purposefully kept her at a distance, and it annoyed her that Jake still blamed her for not telling him about Matthew. He'd seen the letter the lawyer had written her, had proof that it was *his* lawyer's mistake. Apparently, Jake still needed to accept the fact that she'd believed he hadn't wanted anything to do with her, and to Catherine that had meant her son, as well.

"I see you're ready," Jake commented, his intense, dark gaze sliding over her.

Catherine glanced briefly at him, avoiding his eyes and his piercing stare. "Ready as I'll ever be, I guess."

He nodded, then turned his horse around. They rode out of the yard and around the outside of the fenced pasture toward a patch of trees.

"There's a trail through there," he said, pointing to a barely discernible opening.

Catherine glanced over at him. "You want me to ride through there?" she asked, her tone questioning his sanity. The grove of trees he'd pointed to left a lot to Catherine's imagination. She couldn't even see the trail he was pointing at.

"It'll open up more as we go through," he assured her. "Go on," he encouraged. "You won't be sorry."

Catherine wasn't too sure about that, but she did as she was told and started her horse through the trees.

"Watch out for low branches," Jake warned, calling to her.

Catherine nodded. The small path did open up after

a bit, and she had more room to negotiate the trees. She and Flo seemed to be getting along fine, which was a relief. "You promise not to throw me," she whispered to the horse, "and I promise I'll give you a nice treat."

It was dark under the canopy of the trees, and Catherine wondered what wild animals made this their home. She reminded herself to warn Matthew not to come out here on his own.

Even though she had on a sleeveless blouse, she felt a trickle of sweat slide between her breasts. She had to admit that the shade of the trees was a welcome respite from the blazing Texas sun, and she was glad that she'd pulled her hair up into a ponytail and off her neck.

They'd been riding for about fifteen minutes when she saw a clearing up ahead. She turned in her seat a bit to look back at Jake just about the time he called a warning to her. Catherine realized she should have been watching where she was going when she turned back around and was slapped by a tree branch.

"Ouch!" she cried, then put her hand to her neck. Holding it there, she leaned a little forward, trying to catch her breath. She maneuvered Flo into the clearing and managed to bring the horse to a halt.

Despite the pain from the scrape, Catherine couldn't believe the beautiful sight before her. There was a small meadow and beyond it a large lake surrounded by trees and wildflowers.

Jake rode out of the woods and stopped beside her.

"Are you all right?" he asked, and his gaze roamed over her face.

"I'm fine," she insisted, her hand covering the wound. Tears had gathered in her eyes from the stinging sensation, but Catherine wasn't about to mention it.

Jake shook his head impatiently. "Let me see," he demanded.

"It's nothing," Catherine told him, but she didn't move her hand.

"If it's nothing, you'll let me see it," he reasoned. Leaning over, he reached for her hand.

With the little bit of skill she'd acquired, Catherine urged Flo to start walking again. "I'm okay," she called over her shoulder. She was aware of Jake following her, and she led the way over to the lake. She stopped just short of it.

"Is it okay to let them drink?" she asked, looking in his direction.

He nodded sharply as he dismounted. He took the reins from Catherine and held Flo still while she got down from her horse, then turned the animals loose. With a determined expression he faced her.

"Let me see."

"Jake—"

He ignored her protest and stepped closer, grasping her wrist before she had a chance to move away from him. Catherine caught her breath as Jake removed her hand from her neck.

A string of curse words flowed from Jake's mouth as fluidly as hot lava out of a volcano. Several deep, red welts were striped across the side of her neck, and blood had begun to ooze from the worst one. "What in hell did you do to yourself?" He tilted her chin up and to the side, examining her without really expecting an answer.

"It's nothing," Catherine said again, but she winced when he touched her neck with the tip of his finger.

"Dammit," Jake bit out, "I told you to watch out for the branches."

"I was watching out for them—"

"Not very well," Jake barked. "If you'd been paying attention to where you were going, this wouldn't have happened."

Catherine tried to shake his hand free from hers, but Jake didn't let it go. "I only turned around for a moment," she replied, justifying her actions. "I was going to ask you something."

"Well, you should have been watching where you were going." Jake began dragging her under the shade of the trees and Catherine tried to dig in her heels. Her strength proved no match for his.

"What are you doing?" she demanded, struggling to free his hold on her.

"You're bleeding. The cuts need to be cleaned," Jake told her, his tone stern. With his free hand he retrieved a canteen of water from his saddle.

"Here, give it to me. I can do it," Catherine told him. At the moment she was more concerned about Jake's hands on her than how much the cuts hurt.

Jake ignored her. At the edge of the lake he let her go. "Sit down," he said, pointing to the base of a tree.

Catherine refused, and the look she gave him could have melted a snowman on a freezing winter's day. "Jake—"

"Sit," he ordered again.

Catherine shrugged her shoulders and gave up. She watched as Jake pulled a handkerchief from his pocket. He opened the canteen and poured water over the cloth, then twisted out the excess water. He dropped to his knees in front of her.

"Tilt your head up," he instructed, then helped her with a finger under her chin.

To avoid a clash of minds, Catherine obeyed. However, as soon as the cold, wet cloth touched her neck, she yelped.

"It's okay," Jake said soothingly as he gently dabbed at Catherine's neck, wiping away the traces of blood that had collected along the cut. He slid his other hand behind her head to hold her still. "It's just cold."

Catherine nodded. "It startled me," she admitted, and she hoped he didn't notice the huskiness of her tone. His nearness was disturbing enough without his hands on her. She held her breath, both wishing the moment over and wanting him to keep on touching her.

Jake leaned forward to get a closer look at the scrapes. "We're going to have to clean this better when we get back and put some antiseptic on it," he told her, then looked up. Their gazes collided. Heat radiated between them.

Catherine swallowed hard. She'd been dreading, yet anticipating this moment for weeks. There was no way she could pull away from Jake now. If he didn't want her, it would be up to him to back off. She no longer had the strength to keep him at bay.

"Catie."

His message was clear. Nothing more needed to be said. He wanted her and he let her know it, let her see the desire raging inside him. Yet he waited for what seemed like an eternity before he pressed closer.

He didn't kiss her. Instead he lowered his mouth and touched his lips to the tender area of her neck, soothing it with his mouth in a way that a healing cream and a bandage could never do.

"Oh, Jake," Catherine whispered, and the sensations

he made her feel stole her breath. "Jake." She put her hand against his cheek as his tongue slid out and caressed the sensitive area.

Without even thinking about it, Catherine went up on her knees and pressed her body against Jake's. She wanted to guide his mouth to hers, but Jake made slow work of easing the pain from her cut and the result of his ministrations started a burning sensation in the deepest part of her.

Catherine had known it would come to this. She should have been strong enough to resist temptation. But she knew she and Jake shared something special. The years that had passed hadn't changed that.

"Please."

Jake answered her plea by covering her mouth with his. Pleasure soared through her, piercing every nerve along her spine, making her ache for so much more.

Catherine knew that being with Jake like this wasn't in her best interest. A voice was whispering to her to stop things before they went too far, not to let Jake back into her heart. She was taking a chance on getting hurt by this man once again.

Jake drew Catherine against him, and she felt his hardness against her belly. All reasonable thought left her at that moment. He groaned low in his throat as their bodies touched intimately, her breasts grazing his chest. Catherine grasped his shoulders and held on to him as if she were in danger of falling off a cliff. His tongue slid into her mouth, searching, desperately seeking hers.

Catherine couldn't breathe. Jake's kisses seemed to overpower her. She pressed even closer, wanting to feel him against her, to feel the heat of his body seep into her.

Jake tugged at her shirt, yanking it up until he could slide his hand beneath it. He covered her breast, then molded it in his palm, stroking her, sending shafts of heat racing through her.

He pulled away from her, his gaze heavy-lidded with desire. He lowered his hands and locked them around her waist. "I want to see you," he rasped. "Take off your shirt."

His demand didn't shock her. Catherine complied, wanting the same thing. She needed Jake's touch, needed to feel his mouth on her breast. Her gaze remained fixed with his as she slowly unbuttoned her blouse, tantalizing him, enjoying the power she had over him. She slipped the last button free, then prolonged the moment of exposing herself to him by reaching behind her back and unsnapping her bra.

Her breasts were aching now, swelling, yearning to be stroked. Catherine slid her blouse off, then her bra. She put her hands beneath her breasts, lifting them, and Jake lowered his mouth to her, first touching each nipple briefly with a kiss, then grazing them with his teeth.

Catherine hissed as Jake finally settled his attention on one of her breasts. He licked her with his tongue, then sucked her into his mouth. She moaned deeply as his hand covered her other breast, massaging it, then swirling her nipple between his fingers.

"Jake."

It was a cry for more, and Jake's hands slid to her bottom, then intimately pressed her closer. "This is how much I want you, Catie," he admitted. "Tell me you want the same thing," he demanded.

"Yes," she confessed.

Jake eased her down to the soft patch of grass beneath them and covered her body with his own. Catherine's arms slid around his shoulders to the back of his head, holding his mouth to hers.

She trembled in his arms as his hands searched and discovered the softness of her body. Catherine gave herself to the moment, to the ecstasy of being touched by Jake, being intimate with him. Maybe she couldn't have him forever, maybe that wasn't to be, but she was with him now, and she was reveling in his lovemaking.

Jake slipped open the button of her jeans and slid the zipper down, exposing her white silk panties. Catherine lifted her hips as he tugged her pants from beneath her. With ease, Jake removed her shoes, then the remainder of her clothing.

Catherine lay exposed before him, and Jake made quick work of shedding his clothes before lying beside her in the grass. He couldn't believe she was there with him. He ran a finger across her cheek to the base of her throat. She lifted her head, her eyes searching his as he lowered his hand to cup her breast.

Her eyes closed momentarily, then opened again as his hand slid lower, across her abdomen, then lower still. Her hips arched when he touched the core of her, and Jake took his time learning every inch of her body once again.

"Oh, Jake." She whispered his name between her teeth. Her hand slid behind his neck, drawing his mouth to hers. "Kiss me, Jake."

He lowered his head and gently touched her lips, then his mouth rested on hers, feasted on hers, until they were both breathing heavily.

Jake slid over her, his body hard and ready, aching to feel her warmth, to be inside her. Catie opened her legs for him, and Jake slid into her.

"Ah, Catie," he whispered, sinking deeper as the

words left his mouth. "You feel so good." His lips nudged hers as his hips rocked against her. Catherine moaned low in her throat as she returned his kisses.

She spread her legs wider, and Jake gave her more of himself, pushing against her hips. His hands grasped her buttocks, lifting her to him, giving him deeper access.

"Yes," Jake grated, his teeth clenched. "Take all of me, Catie." His hips rocked faster, and he was rewarded by the glazed look in her eyes as her pleasure came to her.

"Oh, Jake…Jake."

Jake lost control, pumping his hips harder and faster until he couldn't think, couldn't comprehend anything except the gratification of being with Catie, of loving her body. He felt himself slipping into a void, and a low growl came from deep inside him as he slipped over the brink of reality into a world of wonder and fulfillment.

In the aftermath, as he lay naked with Catie, Jake could remember many times when he'd made love to this woman. His heart seemed heavy, constricted by the thoughts rushing at him.

What was he thinking, letting things go this far with Catie? He closed his eyes and admonished himself with a few silent words.

"We always were good together, weren't we, Jake?" Catherine whispered.

Jake pulled away and looked down at her. "Catie—"

"Don't you dare apologize, Jake McCall," she warned him, her tone suddenly curt. "Neither of us planned on this, but I'm perfectly capable of handling an affair—"

His sharp look stopped her words. *An affair.* Jake should have been pleased that she was looking at the situation so pragmatically. Apparently she wasn't looking for a commitment. Well, neither was he, so he should have felt relief instead of this odd sense of irritation.

Hell, she was right. They'd always been good in bed.

"I don't know what it is about you, Catie. I take one look at you and my sanity disappears."

He said it grudgingly, already regretting letting Catherine a little closer to his heart. Turning his back to her, he gathered their clothing and handed Catherine hers. He dressed, then watched as Catie finished, her fingers fumbling with the buttons on her blouse.

She was beautiful, bewitching, and Jake knew he was in trouble. His heart thudded heavily in his chest, an ache he couldn't quite identify. He had a gut feeling this was going to end badly...for both of them. Nothing good could come out of them having an affair. Jake had nothing to offer Catie.

That they were still physically attracted to each other didn't mean anything. They only had Matthew in common. They lived different lives in different cities. In a few weeks, Jake reminded himself, Catie would be leaving to go home.

Catherine finished dressing and turned toward him, brushing her hair away from her face with her fingertips. "What did happen, Jake?" she asked quietly.

Jake knew what she was asking. He didn't have an answer for her now, any more than he had the first time they talked. "You know what happened." He said it more brusquely than he intended. He hadn't thought about compromising the situation between them. He should have been thinking about Matthew instead of his mother.

Catie didn't know everything about him, and to Jake's way of thinking she didn't need to. She was still young, still had the chance to find someone to love, get married and have more children. Something Jake couldn't give her.

"You never called me."

Jake buckled his belt, then rested his hands on his hips. "I meant to. I swear I did. There was just so much to do when I got home." He shook his head. "Catie, if I had known about Matthew, I'd have found some way to be there for you." He briefly thought of mentioning the accident, then stopped himself. He just couldn't talk about it with her.

She looked as if she wanted to believe him, but still had doubts. Jake didn't know what to say to convince her. Apparently, she wanted to believe the worst about him. He didn't pretend to know what it had been like for her, raising Matthew on her own.

"How did your parents take it?" he asked, raising a brow in question. "Were they upset when you told them?"

"What do you think?" Catherine answered, her defensive tone giving clue as to her parents' reaction. She tucked her blouse into her pants, then walked to the edge of the lake, away from him.

Jake followed her. "Tell me what happened," he said.

"Oh, you don't want to know." Catherine kept her back to him.

Jake reached out to touch her shoulder, then stopped himself. Just the thought of touching her made him hard, made him want to strip her clothes off and make

love to her again. She'd said she could handle an affair.
It crossed Jake's mind to wonder if he could.

"Tell me, Catie."

She turned to confront him, and all the sorrow of the
past was in her haunted green eyes. "They disowned
me."

It took a moment before he absorbed the shock of
her words. "What?" Jake grated, anger pulling at him.

She twisted her hands back and forth, locking her
fingers together, then separating them again. "I worried
for days about how to tell them. I knew they'd be upset,
that they'd be disappointed." She took a deep breath,
as if she needed it to go on.

"What did they say?" Jake prompted when she
stopped speaking.

"I waited as long as I could before telling them.
Finally, when I got the letter from your attorney, I realized that you weren't going to call me." She sniffed,
then ran a hand through her hair. "As much as I hated
to admit it, I wanted their support. I needed someone
to listen, to reassure me that everything was going to
work out."

She trembled violently, her body visibly shaking.
She held her arms in an effort to control herself. "My
father called me a slut. He said I had no morals and
that God was punishing me for being weak."

"Oh, Catie, I'm sorry." Jake reached toward her,
but before he could touch her, she shrank away from
him.

"I wanted so much for them to be there for me."
Tears came to her eyes and still she held them back.
"Of course I expected them to be upset. I knew my
pregnancy would be shocking, but in my heart I'd
hoped and prayed that my parents would love me, that

they would want to help me.'' She sobbed then, the tears finally breaking through. Her shoulders slumped as she raised her hand to her face, covering it.

''Catie, come here.'' Jake reached for her again, and this time she didn't resist. He pulled her into his embrace and wrapped his arms around her, holding her against him, rubbing her back with his palm. ''I'm so sorry you had to go through that on your own.''

''Jake, they wouldn't even let me see my sisters,'' she told him on a ragged breath. ''They said I was a bad influence, that I didn't deserve to ever talk to them again.'' The tears in her throat stopped her from speaking.

Jake had never met Catie's parents, but from what she'd told him, they were strict, especially her father. He remembered being in the room when Catie talked with her father on the phone, and the times she'd cried afterward.

''Hush, Catie. They can't hurt you now.''

Catherine cried harder as she stood in his arms. All of the years of hurt and pain came rushing at her. She allowed herself the luxury of being held by Jake, of feeling his powerful arms surround her with warmth and strength, something she'd needed for so long.

Finally she sniffed and looked up at him, her eyes swollen with tears. ''Bethany and Sarah would be in their twenties now,'' she commented, her tone filled with sadness. ''I wanted so much to talk to them, to tell them that I loved them, but my father made me leave that day before they came home from school.''

Jake tightened his arms around her. ''I know that must have hurt you.''

Catherine shook her head. ''I never saw them again. I've written them letters, but they've never answered them. I don't know if they don't want to see me or if my father never let them have my letters. After a while the envelopes started coming back unopened. My parents must have moved away.''

Jake ran his hand up to the back of her neck, then his palm cupped her chin, lifting it so he could see her face. ''I'd give anything to be able to go back and change things for you. I want you to believe I would never have let you go through that on your own.''

''It doesn't matter anymore,'' she said, then abruptly pushed out of his arms and away from him. ''I don't know why I told you all that, except that you caught me at a bad moment,'' she insisted. ''I've learned to live with it.''

Jake figured it must have been tough for Catie, but he wasn't ready to let his heart soften toward her. She still hadn't explained why she'd kept Matthew a secret from him.

''Twelve years is a long time, Catie. Don't you think you could have found time to tell me about Matthew during that time?'' She shot him a look then, full of guilt or remorse, he wasn't sure which.

''You know I tried to contact you. I even left messages at your house.''

Jake nodded. ''That was when you first found out?'' he asked pointedly. She nodded. ''What about later? What stopped you from calling me sometime during the twelve years my son was growing up?''

Catherine bit at her bottom lip as she contemplated her thoughts. ''When I got the letter from you—''

''You know I didn't send that letter,'' Jake interrupted, his tone insistent as he began to rebuild his defenses toward her.

''Regardless, Jake, I *thought* you did. You need to

try and understand how I felt. I believed you didn't want anything to do with me. I wasn't going to force myself or my son on you."

Jake looked over at the lake, his expression solemn. "I wish I'd known. I would have been a part of his life. I've missed so much, so many years that I can never get back." Inside, he couldn't seem to let it go.

"I know." Catherine started to touch him, then instinct stopped her.

"Matthew is the most important thing in my life now. I'm not going to let you keep him from me any longer." It sounded like a warning. Jake intended it to. Regardless of the fact that they were attracted to each other, that they'd made love, Jake wasn't going to let anything, or anyone, not even Catie, come between him and his son.

"Oh, Jake, I know that," she whispered. "Whatever happens, I want you and Matthew to spend time together."

Whatever happens. Jake took that statement for what it was worth. If a summer fling was what Catie wanted, he was going to oblige her.

He leaned down and brushed his mouth over hers. The kiss, which began as a light meeting of their lips quickly became much more. Jake had to pull away. Kissing Catie wasn't the only thing he wanted to do with her at that moment.

"I guess we'd better get back before someone comes looking for us."

She licked her lips, then nodded. Together they walked toward the horses who were grazing nearby. Jake made sure Catie had no trouble mounting Flo, then he whistled. His horse obediently trotted over to him, and he swiftly climbed up on him.

Catherine let Jake lead the way, following closely behind him. She'd told Jake that she could handle an affair. Now she just had to prove it. Making love with him had only reassured her of how much she loved him. Was it wrong to relish every moment she could have with him, knowing that in a few weeks she'd be going back home and leaving her heart here?

Catherine sighed deeply. Her heart had been terribly bruised once by this man. She had never expected to fall in love with Jake again.

When they arrived at the barn, Jake dismounted, then held Catie's horse for her. "Let's get you inside," he said. Before they took a step, Matthew came running up to them.

"Hey Mom, Dad, guess what—" He stopped speaking and his eyes widened. "Mom, what happened?" he asked, then darted a questioning look at Jake.

"It's nothing," Catherine said in a rush to reassure her son. "Jake and I were riding through some trees, and a branch hit me. That's all. It needs a little cleaning."

Matthew didn't look quite convinced. "Does it hurt?" he asked, and he looked worried.

Jake was proud of his son at that moment. When Matt had first come to the ranch, he'd been so afraid that Catie would take him home that he was angry with her for a while. Since he learned he could stay for the summer, he'd gradually let down his guard. He was genuinely concerned about his mother.

"We're on our way up to the house to do just that, Matt. How about taking care of the horses for us?"

"Sure." Matt smiled and eagerly took the reins.

Jake and Catherine started for the house. As soon as

they entered, they ran into Lynn. She took one look at Jake and stated, "I swear that man is the most disagreeable, ill-tempered man I've ever had the displeasure of knowing." She yanked off her gloves and slapped them against her thigh.

Jake's gaze darted to Catherine. "Russ."

Catherine's brows lifted as Lynn continued her tirade.

"He thinks he knows everything. *And* he thinks I'm incapable of learning the smallest of tasks. I don't know how much longer I can put up with him. He's so—" Her gaze went to Catherine's neck. "What on earth happened to you?" she cried, her own problem temporarily forgotten.

"I had a run-in with a tree branch while Jake and I were out riding," Catherine stated.

Lynn moved nearer to get a better look. "I'll say you did. That must really hurt."

Catherine nodded, remembering how much it had hurt until Jake had started kissing her and licking it with his tongue. The pain from her cut had been easily forgotten as he'd awakened every sensual nerve ending in her body. She tried not to blush, but her cheeks reddened slightly. "It does," she admitted.

"What's going on?" Ashley asked, coming from the hallway and stopping beside them. She had a baby on each hip.

"Catherine got hurt while riding," Lynn told her, taking one of the babies and cuddling her. She kissed the top of Melissa's head.

Ashley saw the red welts. "Oh, my goodness! Catherine, come into the bathroom, and I'll help you clean that."

Jake grabbed Catherine by the arm. "You look busy.

I'll do it,'' he told the two women. Before they could answer, he dragged Catherine from the room, leaving Lynn and Ashley standing in the foyer with surprised looks on their faces.

''Whoa,'' Lynn commented, raising her blond eyebrows and rolling her eyes. ''Did you get a whiff of that testosterone?'' She grinned.

''Sure did,'' Ashley agreed, smiling. Her gaze met Lynn's. ''The next few weeks should prove to be quite interesting.''

Lynn nodded, and the two women shared a knowing look.

Ten

Catherine heard the shower running in the bathroom between her room and Jake's. It had been over a week since they'd made love, and her body seemed to be craving his. Jake and Ryder had been out with some of the ranch hands hunting a wild animal that had attacked cattle grazing in the north pasture.

Instead of returning home every day, they'd camped out until they'd tracked the animal down. Finally, this evening, they'd rode in, and Catherine had been so relieved to see Jake. Only she hadn't been able to throw her arms around him as Ashley had with Ryder.

Catherine had been worried about Jake, but she'd limited herself to discussing his safety along with that of Ryder's when talking about how dangerous it was to be out with rifles in the dark wilderness.

Ashley and Lynn had assured her that the men were fine, that this was a part of ranch life, but to Catherine's way of thinking, that didn't matter. She'd wanted Jake to come home safely.

Now he was naked in the shower, and she wondered if she was brave enough to do what she was thinking. She quickly unbuttoned her blouse and slipped it off. The rest of her clothes were shed in a hurry, before she lost her nerve.

She'd told Jake she could handle an affair. It didn't matter now whether she could or not. She wanted to be with him, even though they only had a short while before she had to leave. Jake hadn't *seemed* opposed to the idea. If he was, she was going to make a big fool of herself.

With her hand shaking, she tried the bathroom door. Relief washed over her when she realized he hadn't locked it. As she stepped in, steam engulfed her. She took a deep breath, then moved the shower curtain aside.

"Jake?"

"Catie." Jake stepped from beneath the spray, his expression momentarily one of surprise. Shock quickly gave way to desire. His eyes widened appreciatively as he stared at her naked body. He didn't say a word as he held his hand out to her.

Catherine hesitated a moment, her gaze sliding over his hard-muscled chest, down his flat belly, but before she could look further, he reached for her, drawing her into the shower and against him. Water ran freely over them. He was hard against her, making her feel powerful and seductive.

"Ah, Catie," he whispered, then his mouth lowered to hers. Catherine lost her breath as he kissed her deeply. She clung to him as his tongue caressed hers. Erotic thoughts raced through her mind as his hands glided along her back. She sighed with pleasure as he grasped her buttocks and pressed her intimately against him.

"I guess it's okay that I surprised you, huh?" she asked when his mouth finally released hers.

"You can surprise me like this anytime," Jake answered, his voice raw with desire as his gaze met hers. His hand slid up and down her back, sending her nerve endings into a frenzy. "You feel wonderful."

"You do, too." She slipped her hands over his broad shoulders and around his neck as she lifted her lips and placed kisses along his mouth and neck. "I was worried about you," she confessed.

Jake grunted as her tongue grazed his. "It took a lot longer than we thought it would," he told her, capturing her mouth beneath his for a moment, nipping her bottom lip with his teeth. His hand found her breast, and he grazed the hard peak of her nipple with his thumb. "I thought about doing this to you the whole time I was away."

"You did, huh?" she asked, then she moaned when he lowered his mouth and captured her breast with his lips. He sucked on her hungrily.

"Yeah," he answered. "I wanted to touch you like this." He ran his finger down her middle and between her legs. "And like this." He slipped his finger into her and she arched her body against his hand.

"Oh, Jake." Catie felt her world slip a little. Jake had the power to make her wish she could have him for a lifetime. "Mmm, Jake, that feels so good."

"What about this?" he asked. He kissed her other breast, sucking her nipple greedily, then ran his tongue along her belly. He dropped to his knees and looked up at her.

Catie felt her legs go weak. "I think we'd better get out of here before I can't move at all."

"In a minute," he promised. His warm tongue touched her, and Catherine's head fell back as her world exploded right then and there.

"Jake."

After a moment he stood and faced her. "Turn around," he commanded, then helped her with his hands on her shoulders. He kissed her neck as he ran his hands along her rib cage, then cupped her breasts. Catherine pushed against him and he grunted with gratification.

"You're killing me," he whispered in her ear, his tongue slipping out to trace the pink shell. His teeth nibbled her lobe. Her hips rocked back against him and he groaned. "Mmm, Catie, I think you're right." He leaned over and turned the faucet off. "I can't wait much longer. I want to be inside you."

Catherine started to grab a towel, but Jake prevented her. "Let me," he whispered, wrapping a towel around his waist. She stood docilely as he gently rubbed the soft fabric over her body. Never before in her life had Catherine believed that something as simple as drying her body could be so sensually awakening. Her entire being felt as if it was on fire.

Jake dried her hair, then ran the towel down her back. He watched her as he moved it between her legs. Ripples of pleasure shot through her, and Catherine had to brace herself by putting her hands on his shoulders. "Jake, please."

He rose to stand beside her, his gaze locked with hers as he dried the remaining water from his body. He threw the towel to the floor, then pulled her toward him. Before she could say anything, he swept her into his arms and carried her to his bedroom. Together they fell on the bed. Jake rolled over on his back and pulled Catherine on top of him.

Spreading her body over his, Catherine writhed against his manhood, and he hardened even more. She kissed his chest as she raised herself above him. Then he was inside her, and her whole world seem to shatter. There was no buildup of desire, just fireworks rocketing through her body.

Catherine moved her hips, and Jake pushed deeper into her. She sighed as a million lights burst into a display of colors in her mind. Unable to remain upright, she fell across him and his arms surrounded her.

She found his mouth, and their tongues intertwined as Jake grasped her buttocks, his touch urgent as he sought his own release. She shuddered, her body quivering with erotic pleasure as his muscles tensed.

She loved this man with all of her heart. And in a couple of weeks she was going to have to leave him.

"Are you going to take a break all day or do you plan on doing any work?" Jake demanded, his gaze raking his brother Ryder as he leaned casually against the fence post. They'd been repairing the roof on one of the barns for the past two days. At the rate they were going, they'd be at it all day tomorrow unless, as Jake saw it, Ryder got off his butt and started working.

"What the hell is your problem, big brother?" Ryder demanded, casting Jake a sharp, observant look. "You've been as cantankerous as a rodeo bull all morning." He swigged down cold water from a thermos, then capped it.

"Nothing's the matter," Jake denied, his tone biting. Ryder eyed his brother speculatively. "This wouldn't have anything to do with Catherine and Matthew leaving in a few days, would it?"

Jake's gaze met Ryder's. "No, it wouldn't." His denial came too quickly, and his brother arched one brow.

"Yeah, right." Ryder shoved away from the fence and approached Jake. "What are you going to do?"

"About what?" Jake asked, not willing to get into a personal conversation about Catie. The fact that she was leaving soon had been eating at him for the past week. He'd gotten too used to having her around—too used to having her in his bed. They'd managed to make love together every night since that day in the shower. In a houseful of people, that was quite an accomplishment to keep secret.

Exasperated, Ryder took a deep breath. "About Matthew. Are you going to let Catherine take him back to Lubbock?"

"What choice do I have?" Jake said, leaning an arm against the fence. "I asked Catherine to let him stay the summer and she did. I can't ask her to let him live here."

Actually, he'd wrestled with the thought of doing just that. He wanted his son on his ranch. He didn't want another day to pass, when his son would grow and change, without being close enough to enjoy it. Watching Catherine leave was going to be hard enough. He didn't want to lose Matthew, too.

"You could ask Catherine to stay," Ryder commented, then slanted a look in his brother's direction.

"That's not going to happen," Jake stated firmly.

"So you haven't gotten over the fact that she didn't tell you about Matthew?" Ryder asked pointedly.

Jake grunted. "You think I should forget that she kept my son a secret from me for twelve years?"

Sleeping with Catherine, making love to her, hadn't softened Jake's stance on how he felt about her keeping Matthew from him for so long. Jake had tried, really tried, but he couldn't seem to let it go. Just as he couldn't forget about what his father had done.

"What purpose does it serve to continue to be angry about it?" Ryder asked.

Jake glared at his brother. "You don't have any idea what it feels like to have someone lie to you like that."

Ryder tugged at his mustache with his fingers. "Ashley kept her pregnancy a secret from me. I seemed to have learned to live with that," he reminded Jake.

"That isn't the same thing," Jake told him, wondering what Ryder would think, how he'd feel, if he knew the truth about their father. If he did, maybe he would understand why Jake wasn't able to forget, or forgive, what Catie had done.

Ryder frowned. "As I see it, it's exactly the same thing." There was something in his brother's eyes, a deep sadness that Ryder didn't think had anything to do with Catherine. "What aren't you telling me?" he asked.

Jake turned his back and started to pick up a piece of plywood. "Lay off. You don't want to know."

Without meaning to, Jake had piqued Ryder's curiosity. "What the hell is eating at you? It's more than what Catherine did, isn't it?" he pressed. Jake didn't say anything, and Ryder swore. "Dammit, Jake, talk to me."

Jake swung around and faced Ryder. "I'm not your brother—only your half brother," he stated harshly. All the hurt and anguish Jake had been feeling for years was revealed in his dejected tone.

Ryder shook his head, confusion forming his expression. His eyes questioned Jake's statement. "Now I know you're losing it, big brother."

Jake murmured, "It's the truth, Ryder. I didn't mean for you to find out this way."

Ryder looked at Jake as if he had two heads. "What in the devil are you talking about?"

Jake was quiet for a minute, then he said, "I didn't want you to know. I still don't want you to—" He hesitated, then gave in to Ryder's determined expression. There wasn't any way to get out of this now. "I know this is going to hurt, and I don't mean to do that." He waited a moment, then stated, "Dad had an affair with a woman who lived in San Antonio while he was married to Mom. Apparently, the woman got pregnant with me."

"You're crazy. Where did you hear that?" Ryder demanded. His hands coiled into fists.

"It's true," Jake said, aware that his brother was seething. Jake knew how he felt. He'd experienced the same kind of rage when he'd found out. It would be even harder for Ryder to understand. He had shared a special bond with their mother.

"Mom wouldn't have stood for that."

"Apparently Mom did."

Ryder swung at him then, and Jake dodged his blow, blocking it with his arm. He shoved Ryder away, hard enough to knock him into the fence. "It's the truth. I found it out when I took over the ranch. There were papers explaining everything, and a legal adoption by Mom," he explained, his voice rising. "I didn't want to believe it, either," he confessed.

Ryder looked stunned as he straightened and faced Jake. He didn't say anything.

"It makes sense, Ryder, when you think about it. I

don't look like you or Deke or Lynn. You've all got blond hair, and mine's brown. Your eyes are blue, mine are dark-brown. Think about it," he stated defensively. "It's true. I guess they never intended to tell us."

"Who else knows about this?" Ryder demanded.

"Just me, now that Frank Davis is dead. And my biological mother, whoever and wherever she is." He bit his lip, then said, "I don't want Lynn or Deke to know."

Ryder swore, then took a deep breath. "If it's true," he began slowly, as if he still doubted it, "what difference does it make? You're our brother and you always will be."

Jake just looked at him, his jaw tight.

"Damn, Jake, did you think this would matter to me or Lynn or Deke?" he asked. From his brother's expression, it was apparent that Jake had worried about exactly that. "We have the same McCall blood running through our veins. You're our brother, for heaven's sake!"

Jake said nothing, and Ryder swore again. "Even knowing about this, you took care of us. If you loved us enough to do that, how can you even *think* that we'd feel differently about you?"

"I don't know." Jake shook his head. "It was a hell of a thing to learn after Mom and Dad died."

"I guess that's so, but it doesn't change anything. I mean it." He put his hand on his brother's shoulder. "You've been carrying this around for years," he commented. "Is that why you've been so hard on Catherine?" Ryder asked.

Jake didn't say anything. He knew Ryder was right—he just couldn't admit as much.

"So you're punishing her for Dad's indiscretion?"

"That's not what I'm doing," Jake told him. "But I can't let myself trust her again."

Ryder glared at Jake. "You're going to just let her walk out of your life?"

Jake favored his brother with a hard look. "I'm not *letting* her do anything. She doesn't live here. She doesn't want to live here."

"Are you sure about that?"

Jake grunted. "She's going back to Lubbock. I'm not going to stand in her way."

"Even if it means that she'll be taking Matthew with her?" Ryder persisted.

Jake looked over the fence at his son, who was out riding in the pasture. "Damn, I'm going to miss him." His voice was strained.

"Then don't let him go," Ryder told his brother. When Jake said nothing, Ryder continued, "Look, I'm no idiot. I've seen the way you look at Catherine and the way she looks at you."

Jake glared at him. "Mind your own business."

"You're going to tell me you don't care if she leaves?"

"I'm not going to tell you anything. Let's get back to work."

Ryder swore. "You're dumber than you look."

Jake sat at the desk in the office and tried to think about anything except the fact that Catie was leaving tomorrow. It wasn't as simple as Ryder made it out to be. Catie was ready to go home. She'd mentioned that she was leaving several days ago. She had a job, a life in Lubbock.

Jake had no right to ask her to stay. As Jake saw it, he had two choices. He could fight Catie for Matthew, or he could accept a custody agreement that would allow him to see his son on school breaks and during the summers.

Jake didn't want to let Matthew go. They'd become close over the summer. It did a little something to Jake's heart every time his son called him Dad. Matthew was the only child Jake would ever have. He couldn't contain the pride that made his chest swell when Matthew looked at him as if he could move mountains.

Catie was the problem. Jake wandered over to the window and looked out. He was immediately aware of the ache in his chest as he watched her talking to Russ. Ryder was wrong. It was lust, not love, he felt for Catie. He couldn't love her. He couldn't *afford* to love any woman.

He had nothing to offer Catie. She was young and vibrant and still had a yearning for life and all it entailed. Over the summer Jake had watched her change. While living on the ranch had come easily to Ashley, Catie had had to work at accepting things moving at a slower pace. She'd seemed happy enough, though, living on the ranch for the summer. Probably because she knew it was temporary.

Jake moved away from the window when he saw Catie heading toward the house. He walked over and stopped in the doorway of the office. His chest grew heavy as she stepped into the hallway.

"Catie."

Catherine smiled when she saw Jake. "Hi." Her heart sped into high gear just at the sight of him.

Jake frowned. "I'd like to speak with you for a minute."

"Sure." For a reason she couldn't state, that one

sentence sounded ominous to her. Catherine tried very hard to keep her breathing steady. This past week had been the hardest in her life. She'd let herself hope that Jake had come to terms with why she'd kept Matthew a secret from him. She'd even let herself dream of them making a life together.

She and Matthew could be happy living on Jake's ranch with all of his family. Though it still hurt that she'd been rejected and disowned by her parents and sisters, Catherine felt so much love and acceptance from the McCall clan. In her heart she secretly harbored the wish that Jake loved her as much as she loved him. The foreboding look on his face, the stern expression in his eyes, warned her that she was living in a dreamworld.

Jake nodded. "Come on in."

Catherine walked through the door, and he slowly closed it. With trepidation, she watched him circle the desk and stand behind it, as if to put distance between them.

"What's the matter, Jake?" she asked, trying very hard to keep herself calm. She moved closer to the desk. Something was about to happen that Catherine felt she wasn't going to like. She could sense it from Jake's distant manner.

He stood quietly looking at her, his expression determined. Then, without blinking, he stated, "I want to keep Matthew here on the ranch with me."

"What?" Catherine didn't exactly understand. Then she figured that he meant until school started. "I wish he could stay a while longer, really I do, but there's a lot to do to get him ready for the beginning of the school year. We have to go back now or else I'd never get everything done."

Even though over the past few weeks they'd become lovers, Jake hadn't made any reference to their relationship becoming permanent. Though Catherine loved Jake, she had her pride. She wasn't going to make a fool of herself and confess her love for him. She had to accept that he didn't love her. Sure, they were still good together in bed, but apparently to Jake that was all she meant to him.

Jake put his hands on his hips. "You don't understand. I want to keep him here permanently."

Catherine swayed, his words knocking her off balance. Her mouth fell open as she stared at him with disbelief. "Oh my, oh, no—" she squared her shoulders "—you want to take him from me." The realization hit her like a heat wave. "I let him come here for the summer so you could get to know each other. I never dreamed—" Her eyes clouded with pain. "This is how you repay me?"

Jake didn't say anything. It was exactly what he'd intended when she'd agreed to let Matthew stay at the ranch for the summer.

"What have you told Matthew?" she demanded. "Did you tell him you were going to keep him here?"

"I haven't said anything to Matthew yet. I wanted to talk it out with you first."

"Talk it out? Well, you can't have him, Jake. How's that for talking it out?" Her eyes darkened, her pupils becoming as black as thunderclouds.

"I'd hoped it wouldn't come to a fight between us," Jake returned roughly.

He'd caught her off guard. She'd never expected him to betray her trust like this. She'd done her part by agreeing to spend the summer on the ranch. This wasn't fair! Her jaw locked as she clamped her teeth together. Finally she took a deep breath, then spoke.

"What? You thought I'd just give up my son without a fight?" Then a horrible thought dawned on her. She'd been such a fool! "Is that what sleeping with me was all about?" she demanded, remembering the way she'd so easily given herself to him. "Was it your plan all along to get me into bed? Did you think that it would be that simple—that for a summer fling I'd let you have my son?"

She began trembling, her body shaking with fury. Her eyes filled with fire. She opened her mouth to speak, clamped it shut again, then turned her back on him and marched toward the door.

Jake started after her. "Catie, wait!"

She stopped, then whirled around to face him. "Leave me alone, Jake." She hated the tears that came then. And she hated the tremor in her voice. She'd have given anything to have appeared strong, instead of on the edge of breaking down.

He frowned at her, and she turned her back to him again. Jake grabbed her arm and made her face him, and she tried to jerk away. She was so angry, so hurt. She looked pointedly at his hand on her arm.

"Take your hand off me."

Jake did, but he didn't move away from her. "I didn't want to do it this way. I never meant to hurt you," he claimed.

"Well, you failed miserably!" she retorted. "If you think I'm giving up my son without a fight, you're mistaken," she cried, her voice vibrating, her throat aching. "I'll fight you with everything I own," she promised. "I swear to you, Jake McCall, in the long run you may win, but I'll die trying to keep Matthew."

Catherine jerked open the door and hurriedly left the office. As she was going down the hallway, she brushed past Ashley without speaking. She couldn't talk to anyone at the moment. She was likely to break down and cry. Jake had hurt her more than she'd ever dreamed possible. She'd trusted him when he'd said he only wanted Matthew to come to the ranch for the summer. All along he'd had other motives—plans to take Matthew from her.

Catherine entered her room in a flurry and rushed to pack her clothes. She was leaving this ranch. Now, before Jake or anyone tried to stop her. And she was taking her son.

Fuming, she threw what she'd brought with her in her suitcase without thought or reason. She would ask Ryder to drive her and Matthew to the airport. If he refused, she'd take one of their damned cars!

What a complete fool she'd been to trust Jake. She had to get away, to distance herself from Jake mentally as well as physically. She'd found it so easy to talk to him, to lean on him, to let him close. Then, without warning, he'd walked on her heart.

Any hope that Jake had feelings for her died the moment he'd told her that he was planning to fight her for Matthew. He couldn't care for her and hurt her like that.

She'd told Jake that she could handle an affair. Well, that's what it had been, no matter how she tried to sugarcoat it. Foolishly she'd let her heart get in the way of her good sense. Now she was going to pay for it.

Jake hadn't really wanted her. He'd wanted Matthew.

"What's going on?" Ashley asked, bewildered. Jake was standing in the doorway, staring after Catherine as she disappeared down another hallway. "Is Catherine all right?" She took one look at Jake, and asked, "What did you say to her?"

"I told her I want to keep Matthew." Jake went back into the office. Ashley followed him.

"You didn't!"

"I've missed the first twelve years of his life. I want him here on the ranch with me. He likes it here. He'll want to stay," Jake insisted.

"Maybe for a while, because this is all so new to him. But eventually he'll miss his mother, Jake."

"We'll work out some kind of custody agreement."

"It didn't sound to me as if you're going to work out anything," Ashley commented. "Catherine was really upset."

Jake looked away. "I can't help that."

"Oh, please." Ashley gave him one of her knowing looks. "Well, did you bother to tell Catherine how you feel about her?"

Jake's gaze swung back to Ashley, but he didn't answer. He sat behind the desk busying himself, making an effort to not give away his thoughts. His sister-in-law didn't give him the opportunity to ignore her. She marched over to him and stood in front of the desk.

"Jake."

"Ashley—"

She put her hands on her slightly rounded hips. "You love her, don't you?"

That brought Jake's gaze to hers again. He didn't deny it, but he didn't admit to it, either. Apparently, that didn't matter to Ashley.

"Jake McCall, have you lost what good sense God gave you?" she demanded.

Jake returned her stare, his brows drawn together. "You seem to think so," he returned flatly.

Letting out a frustrated groan, Ashley leaned over the desk and placed her hands flat on it. "Are you telling me that you don't love Catherine?" she asked, lowering her voice in a way that made Jake feel like a trapped animal. "Jake, anyone with eyes could tell what was going on with you two over the summer."

Jake had thought that he and Catherine had been very discreet. It was disconcerting to find out differently, first from Ryder, now from Ashley. "It's complicated," he said defensively. How he felt about Catie wasn't the issue. She was better off without him.

Ashley didn't let him off the hook. "Well, suppose you explain it to me."

Jake looked away and shuffled some papers in front of him. "You know I have nothing to offer her." Jake wasn't used to discussing personal matters about himself. And he damn sure didn't like where this conversation was going. Ashley, it seemed, wasn't going to give up.

"That's the most pathetic excuse—" she began, then caught herself before continuing. "Oh, Jake," she whispered on a sigh. Ashley's gaze softened as she lowered her voice. "This is about your sterility, isn't it? Did you even discuss it with Catherine?"

Jake's chest tightened. "It's not up for discussion," he returned, his voice hardening a fraction.

Ashley straightened and put her hand on her back. "It's why you're letting her leave."

"Catherine's still very young. She can have other children if she wants. I won't trap her in a relationship she'll likely regret."

"How do you know she wants more children? Did you talk with her about it?"

"No, I didn't," Jake answered irritably. "And I'm not going to. And I'm not talking about this any longer." He stood and reached for his hat. "I've got some things to do. I'll be back later."

"Jake—"

"End of discussion, Ashley," he stated, his tone sharp. He gave her a half-apologetic look. "I mean it."

He stalked to the door and walked out.

Eleven

Jake walked outside the house just in time to see Matthew disappear inside the barn. Stepping off the porch, he headed in the same direction, thinking about asking his son if he wanted to go riding. Matt would jump at the chance. He loved riding that much, seemed to love living at the ranch.

"Hey, son." Matthew looked in his direction as Jake walked inside the barn.

"Dad!" Matthew smiled happily.

"Wanna go for a ride?" Jake asked, already knowing the answer.

"Sure," Matthew agreed quickly. "Can we ask Mom, too?"

The pressure in Jake's chest tightened, causing it to ache. He wasn't surprised by Matt's request. The three of them had gone riding several times lately. "Not this time. How about if it's just us guys?" he suggested.

"Great."

Together they saddled the horses, then a short while later they rode around the corral and toward an open pasture. Jake's heart ached with devotion. He'd never known how much a man could love a child until he'd had a chance to know his son.

They chatted as they rode, but that didn't keep Jake's mind from returning to his argument with Catie. He hadn't meant to hurt her. His motives had been selfish, he knew. But he wanted nothing more than to have Matthew with him all the time, to be an integral part of his son's life.

That Jake wanted Catie also wasn't debatable. He would be a fool if he tried to convince himself otherwise. Somehow, to his way of thinking, Jake had hoped that he could keep his son and still not hurt Catie.

He told himself that he was doing the right thing letting Catie go. She deserved so much more than what he could offer her. She'd had a hard life, and she didn't deserve more heartache.

Many years ago they'd been in love and probably would have married. Jake had never dreamed that he would have the chance, temporarily, to be with Catie again.

And he'd never meant to fall in love with her again.

He glanced at his son. Matthew was happy living here. He would probably want to stay, if given the choice of remaining at the ranch or returning to Lubbock. The boy hardly mentioned his friends or his life in the city. He loved his new baby cousins.

What Ashley said flitted through Jake's mind. Would Matthew want to lose his mother in the bargain? Would his son grow to hate him because Jake had hurt Catie? Jake had learned that his son was very protective of her. That was natural, since it had been just the two of them for a long time.

Jake could have his son, but at what cost? Though he wasn't able to tell Catie how much she meant to him, Jake couldn't deny his feelings for her.

And he couldn't take Matthew from her. Admitting to himself that he was in love with Catie, Jake knew he would sacrifice his own wants, his own desires, for her.

After a while Jake said, "I guess we'd better be getting back."

Matthew nodded and turned in the direction of the house. Jake watched his son, who seemed as comfortable on a horse as if he'd been riding all his life. He had McCall blood.

"I'm going to miss you," Jake said, knowing what he had to do. He would have to be the one to take the heat from Matthew. Jake felt the need to protect Catie. It was the last thing he could do for her.

Matthew looked at his father, his brows angled, his expression confused. Jake had known this would be hard, but he wasn't prepared for the way his own heart ached at the thought of letting his son go. "You know you have to leave with your mom."

"Can't we stay here?" Matthew asked, and there was the blind hope of a child's wishes in his green eyes.

"I'm afraid not," Jake answered. "Your mom has a job in Lubbock. You knew that your visit here was just for the summer," he reminded him.

Matthew shook his head. "But I don't want to go. You could ask Mom to stay here," he said hopefully. "Then we could live together like a family."

Jake's heart ached for his son. He didn't want to hurt

him. "We're not a family, Matthew," he said. "Your Mom's leaving and it's time for you to go, too. But I want you to know how much I love you, and I want you to come here whenever you're not in school. Your mom and I will work out a schedule."

Matthew's eyes teared. "Don't you want me to stay?" he asked.

"That's not possible," Jake told his son. "You have to leave with your mom."

"Then you don't care about me!" Matthew shouted. "I thought you loved me, but you don't!"

"Matthew—" Before Jake could say anything, Matthew kicked his heels against his horse and the animal took off. Knowing his son was in control of the horse, Jake watched him ride back toward the barn. Slowly he headed in the same direction.

"You're leaving now?" Jake asked when he saw Catie's bags packed and sitting on the edge of the bed. He stepped into the room. He took his hat off and held it in his hands.

Catherine stiffened when she heard Jake's voice, and her heart tripped over itself. She wanted so much to tell him that she loved him, but she held back, reminding herself of this man's power to hurt her. She couldn't bear to be rejected by him again.

"I called the airline and booked a flight for late this afternoon. Ryder said he would drive us to the airport." She looked away and fingered the handle of her suitcase. "Ashley and Lynn offered to pack Matthew's computer and things and send them to us." Moments passed as she waited for Jake to speak.

"Catie, I won't fight you for Matt," he finally said. "I talked with him a while ago. He's pretty upset."

"I know. He came in crying." Tears sprang to Catherine's eyes. She knew what it cost Jake to make that decision. He was giving in, letting her have Matthew. Her son had come in from riding, angry at his father. Catherine had talked to him, had tried to make him understand that they couldn't stay here. He blamed his father. That had to hurt Jake.

"I don't know what to say, except thank you from the bottom of my heart. Matthew will be all right after a few days. Give him time to come around." She sniffed, then touched a finger to her eyes.

"I want him to come here as often as possible—that is, if he still wants to see me."

She nodded, her throat constricted from holding back a sob. She drew a deep breath and managed to choke out, "Oh, Jake, of course he will." She ran her fingers through her hair, pushing it away from her face.

Jake slapped his hat against his thigh. "I guess that's it, then." He turned to leave.

Catherine watched him walk toward the door. She loved Jake so much, more than she'd ever dreamed possible. In her heart she felt he had to care for her. Was he really going to let her go?

Please tell me you love me.

But he didn't stop when her heart called out to him. She had to stifle a cry of anguish as he walked out of her life.

"We're going to miss you so much," Ashley said, then hugged Catherine, holding her tight for a moment.

"I can't believe you're leaving," Lynn added. "You're going to come back, aren't you?" she asked, giving Catherine a hug, also.

Catherine drew a breath, then blinked back tears. "I

don't know, but I'm going to miss you all." She patted
Ashley's rounded belly. "You'll let me know?" She
smiled tearfully.

"I'll call you. I promise," Ashley assured her.

Catherine glanced over her shoulder. Ryder and Matthew were waiting at the car. "I'd better go." Unable
to stop herself, she looked down the hallway. Her heart
was at war with itself. She wanted to leave before she
saw Jake again, but she also wished for one last look
at him.

Reluctantly Catherine turned and went outside and
got in the car, shutting the door behind her. She didn't
look back, couldn't bear to. She was leaving her heart
with Jake.

"All set, darlin'?" Ryder asked.

Catherine nodded. She looked at her son. He was
slumped down in the back seat, a sullen expression on
his face. Well, she knew how Matthew felt. She loved
Jake, as well. It was too bad that he didn't care for her
in the same way.

Most of the ride to San Luis was made in silence.
She and Ryder made quiet conversation, but to Catherine it felt forced. All of her thoughts were on Jake.

Ryder was nice enough to check her baggage
through, then walked to the departure gate with her.
They waited in silence for about an hour, until Catherine and Matthew's flight was called. Before saying
goodbye, Ryder gave Catherine a reassuring look.

"You hang in there, darlin'," he told her, putting
his arm around her shoulders. "My brother's pretty
stubborn. All of the McCalls are, and that's a fact."
He grimaced at the fresh tears that came to her eyes.
"Don't give up on him."

Catherine nodded, but she'd already given up any

hope of Jake loving her. If he cared for her, if he loved her, he wouldn't have let her leave. She watched as Ryder ruffled his nephew's hair. Matthew threw his arms around his uncle and clung to him until Catherine told her son it was time to go.

"Thank you for everything," Catherine told Ryder, hugging him again. "I wish—" She stopped herself before speaking what was in her heart.

"Be careful what you wish for, darlin'," Ryder told her, then he winked.

Catherine forced herself to return his smile, then she and Matthew boarded the aircraft.

In the time it took to take the flight from San Luis to Lubbock, Catherine tried not to think about Jake or how much she missed him. She'd been unsuccessful. The memories of being with Jake, lying in his arms, making love with him, taunted her. If only...no, she wasn't going to go down that road.

Jake didn't love her. Catherine had to accept that, and she would have to find a way to put her life back together. She was going to be seeing Jake occasionally when he came for Matthew. Somehow she would have to get past the hurt and go on living.

She'd done it once before when he'd left her pregnant and alone. She was stronger now, she told herself. She would find a way to get over the pain of Jake's rejection. She'd have to for Matthew.

When the plane landed, Catherine and Matthew walked off and entered the terminal. She was looking down at Matthew, talking to him, when he suddenly screamed, "Dad!"

Catherine's gaze swung up and her steps froze. *Jake!*

He was standing across the small corridor, leaning casually against the wall, much like the time he'd come to the airport in San Luis months ago to pick her up. Her breath caught in her throat, and the air in her lungs expanded.

What was he doing here?

Matthew darted over to his father, and Catherine was aware that her son's anger with Jake seemed to be no longer an issue. He was so happy to see him. He threw his arms around Jake and hugged his waist. Jake dipped his head and looked at his son, his hat preventing her from seeing his expression. Catherine's heart ached for them both as she watched them embrace. She was so glad that Matthew wasn't going to stay angry with Jake, but she hadn't realized how hard it was to see him again so unexpectedly.

Somehow she found the strength to approach them. As she came closer, Jake looked at her, and their gazes collided.

"Catie."

"Jake."

Jake studied Catie's expression, looking for any sign that she was glad to see him. Instead, her eyes questioned his presence. Well, he deserved that, he supposed. He'd let her leave the ranch. Now he was here to beg her to come back.

He'd thought that once she and Matthew were gone, he would be able to go back to being the man he was before. That wasn't possible any longer, because that man no longer existed. Catie hadn't been gone very long before Jake had realized that letting her go wasn't an option.

He'd gone to her room, and memories of them together surrounded him. Her perfume had lingered in the air, taunting him, reminding him of her. She'd left a few items of clothing on the bed. Jake hadn't sat there long before deciding to go after her in his plane.

He hoped he wasn't too late.

Jake took his eyes off Catie long enough to ask Matthew to go and watch for their luggage to be unloaded. "Go on," he said, "we'll be there in a few minutes." Matthew was eager to please his father and agreed.

"Don't go anywhere else," Catherine called after him.

Matthew frowned at his mother. "I won't, Mom," he answered in a tone that said he was old enough to handle the task given to him.

Jake turned to look at Catie. She was regarding him with a wariness that he felt was deserved. He put his hand on her shoulder and ushered her to a quiet area, out of the path of other passengers.

"Jake, what are you doing here?" Catherine asked, looking shocked and wary.

"I wanted to talk to you," he said quietly, and he watched her expression for any sign that she hadn't given up on him.

"You could have done that back at the ranch," she returned, stating the obvious.

"I know." Jake was feeling a little foolish now. Catie didn't act happy or relieved to see him. He might have come to see her for nothing. He cleared his throat, looked away, then turned his gaze on her face. His stomach began to churn.

Catherine cocked her head and looked at him, her expression guarded. "Well?"

"I know I hurt you. I didn't mean to, but I did."

"Yes, you did," she agreed, her heart aching.

"I'm sorry."

Catherine nodded. "Thank you for saying so," she answered coolly.

Jake grimaced, his jaw tightening. This was harder than he'd ever imagined. "Are you sorry about the time we spent together?" he asked.

"We never made each other any promises," she said quietly, watching him.

Her lips trembled slightly. It was the first sign that she wasn't as calm and collected as she appeared. Jake tossed his hat in his hands like a big round Frisbee. "Maybe we should have," he told her, and his heart stopped beating.

Her eyes widened slightly. "What?"

Jake reached out and ran his palm along Catie's cheek. "I tried to do the right thing. I thought I could let you go, but I can't." He waited a moment, then whispered, "I love you, Catie."

"Jake—"

He forestalled what sounded to him like a protest with his finger to her lips. "Wait. Don't say anything yet. Please, just listen to me." She nodded and waited, her eyes watching him. "I was angry with you for a long time for keeping Matthew from me. But I held on to that anger because I knew right here," he touched his chest where his heart was beating hard, "that I was falling in love with you."

"You were?" Catherine's gaze softened.

"I thought I could settle for having you beneath me in bed for a while," he admitted, then shrugged. "It was easier to let myself believe that sex with you was enough. That way I could have you, and it didn't matter that you were leaving at the end of the summer."

Catherine swallowed and licked her lips. She stared at him silently.

"I was a fool, Catie. I'm so in love with you that I couldn't stand to be without you when you left."

"Do you mean that?" she asked, sounding as though she didn't quite believe him. "Really, Jake?"

He nodded, then caressed her face with his fingers.

"Oh, Jake, I love you, too. So much." She smiled at him, excited and breathless. She moved into his arms, and Jake pulled her tight against him.

Jake lowered his lips, then settled his mouth on hers. He kissed her with all the passion pent up inside him. Her arms went around him, and her hands, warm and gentle, settled on his neck. Lifting his head, Jake looked into her eyes.

"There's a lot you don't know, a lot we need to talk about," he told her. Unaware that they were getting curious stares from other passengers, Jake kissed her again, not wanting to let her go.

"Nothing matters except that we love each other," Catherine whispered, sighing with happiness.

"This is important. You have to know everything." Jake stiffened and set her away from him. He hesitated, glancing away. Then he took a deep breath and turned his gaze on her. "I can't give you any more children," he grated.

"Jake—"

"No. Listen. There was an accident years ago. When I returned to the ranch after my parents died. I can't have children."

Catie stared at him. "You can't?" she asked.

"No." Jake swallowed hard.

"And you thought that would make a difference to me?" she asked.

"Of course. You're young enough to have more

children. You work with them, so you obviously love kids.''

"Oh, Jake, the only thing that truly matters is that you love me. I've never given thought to having more children. I never thought I'd fall in love again.''

"Are you sure?'' Jake asked, wanting to believe her.

"I'm sure.'' She looked into his eyes. "I love you, Jake McCall, with all my heart. I always will.''

Jake kissed her lips lightly, then gazed into her eyes. "In that case, will you marry me?''

Catherine cocked her head at him, then grinned with delight. "I thought you'd never ask.''

Epilogue

"**Y**ou look beautiful," Lynn told Catherine, admiring her ivory satin dress and matching lace veil. "I'm so happy for you and Jake."

Catherine smiled dreamily. "I've loved your brother with all my heart for so long. I can't believe we're finally getting married." They'd planned an intimate family wedding, which included anyone who lived or worked on the Bar M. Both she and Jake hadn't wanted to wait to plan a big wedding.

"*I* can't believe Jake is getting married!" Lynn stated, then grinned. "Maybe now that he's going to have a family of his own, he'll stop trying to run my life."

"He cares about you, Lynn. He wants what's best for you. You know, when your parents died, he didn't even think about himself or his education or what he was giving up to raise you and your brothers. He knew it was his responsibility to make sure his siblings were taken care of." Jake had told her of his father's secret, though he'd yet to share it with Lynn or Deke.

Lynn nodded. "And we love him for it. But we're really happy that he found you and Matthew. He deserves to be happy, too."

A knock sounded at the door, and they both turned in unison. "Yes?" Catherine called as Lynn went to crack it open.

Ryder poked his head around the edge of the door. "It's time, darlin'."

Catherine couldn't control the butterflies flitting around in her stomach. She'd waited for this moment forever. "I'm ready."

Lynn checked Catherine's dress one last time before leading the way out the door. She'd agreed to be Catherine's maid of honor. Catherine had pleaded with Ashley to be in the wedding, as well, but she'd patted her growing belly and insisted there was no way she would parade around six months pregnant in a formal dress.

Ryder held out his arm to Catherine, and they slowly walked down the hall, then stopped at the doorway to the family room. It had been decorated with an abundance of white ribbons and an array of flowers and greenery. Though it was lovely, to Catherine it really didn't matter where she was married. She'd have been thrilled to marry Jake anywhere, just so long as she could be with him the rest of her life.

Her gaze swept the room, and her heart swelled when she spotted her sister, Bethany. As a wedding gift, Jake had secretly hired an investigator to search for Catherine's siblings, then had flown her sister to the ranch for the wedding. Their youngest sister, Sarah, hadn't been able to come, but Catherine had chatted with her on the telephone, and they were both looking forward to a reunion.

After a long, heart-wrenching talk with Bethany, Catherine had learned that her sisters had never received any of her letters, that their father had told his younger daughters that Catherine had moved and left no way to contact her. Neither sister had known how much Catherine had longed to see them.

As she waited for the wedding march to begin, Catherine's heartbeat quickened. In a corner of the room, Michelle and Melissa babbled with each other in their playpen, oblivious to the ceremony. Ashley had wanted to have the wedding when the girls were asleep, but Catherine wouldn't hear of it. She wanted the entire McCall family present, for they were her family now.

There were quite a few of the ranch hands and their families present, also. Catherine spotted Russ Logan over in a corner, watching from a distance, as if he didn't belong or didn't want to be there, she wasn't sure which.

Ryder had taken his place beside Ashley, and Matthew stood proudly between his father and Deke. Her son had been thrilled to learn that his parents were going to marry and they'd be living at the ranch. Jake had his son's name changed, and Matt had already been registered for the upcoming school year as Matthew McCall.

The music began, and tears of joy formed in Catherine's eyes as her gaze met Jake's. In his dark suit he was so handsome. Just looking at him stole her breath. His gaze remained steadfastly on her as she stopped beside him, and Catherine felt his love flow through her. He reached for her hand and enclosed it in his, and she moved closer, wanting to feel his warmth. "I love you," she whispered.

Jake's heart felt as if it was going to burst. Catie's eyes shone with love as she stood beside him, and he was happier than he'd been in his entire life.

A hush fell over the room as the minister began the ceremony, but Jake was only aware of Catie's presence next to him. He steadfastly repeated his vows to love, honor and cherish her. For Jake, those vows were sacred.

Catie's voice was sure and strong as she spoke. Jake waited until the minister said, "I now pronounce you man and wife," then claimed Catie as his wife with a passionate kiss.

Lifting his mouth, he whispered, "I love you," then he slipped his arm around Catie and drew her tightly against him.

"I love you." Catie smiled at him.

Together they gestured for Matt to join them, and Jake gathered his son close to his side, his heart swelling with pride.

This was his family.

*   *   *   *   *

#1 *New York Times* bestselling author

NORA ROBERTS

brings you more of the loyal and loving, tempestuous and tantalizing Stanislaski family.

Coming in February 2001

The Stanislaski Sisters
Natasha and Rachel

Though raised in the Old World traditions of their family, fiery Natasha Stanislaski and cool, classy Rachel Stanislaski are ready for a *new* world of love....

And also available in February 2001 from Silhouette Special Edition, the newest book in the heartwarming Stanislaski saga

CONSIDERING KATE

Natasha and Spencer Kimball's daughter Kate turns her back on old dreams and returns to her hometown, where she finds the *man* of her dreams.

Available at your favorite retail outlet.

Silhouette®
Where love comes alive™

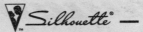

where love comes alive—online...

shop eHarlequin

- ♥ Find all the new Silhouette releases at everyday great discounts.
- ♥ Try before you buy! Read an excerpt from the latest Silhouette novels.
- ♥ Write an online review and share your thoughts with others.

reading room

- ♥ Read our Internet exclusive daily and weekly online serials, or vote in our interactive novel.
- ♥ Talk to other readers about your favorite novels in our Reading Groups.
- ♥ Take our Choose-a-Book quiz to find the series that matches you!

authors' alcove

- ♥ Find out interesting tidbits and details about your favorite authors' lives, interests and writing habits.
- ♥ Ever dreamed of being an author? Enter our Writing Round Robin. The Winning Chapter will be published online! Or review our writing guidelines for submitting your novel.

January 2001
TALL, DARK & WESTERN
#1339 by Anne Marie Winston

February 2001
THE WAY TO A RANCHER'S HEART
#1345 by Peggy Moreland

March 2001
MILLIONAIRE HUSBAND
#1352 by Leanne Banks
Million-Dollar Men

April 2001
GABRIEL'S GIFT
#1357 by Cait London
Freedom Valley

May 2001
THE TEMPTATION OF
RORY MONAHAN
#1363 by Elizabeth Bevarly

June 2001
A LADY FOR LINCOLN CADE
#1369 by BJ James
Men of Belle Terre

MAN OF THE MONTH

For twenty years Silhouette has been giving
you the ultimate in romantic reads. Come join
the celebration as some of your favorite authors
help celebrate our anniversary with the most
sensual, emotional love stories ever!

Available at your favorite retail outlet.

Where love comes alive™